# LOOKING
## for GROUP

### RORY HARRISON

HARPER TEEN

An Imprint of HarperCollinsPublishers

HarperTeen is an imprint of HarperCollins Publishers.

Looking for Group
Copyright © 2017 by Rory Harrison
All rights reserved. Printed in the United States of America.

ISBN 978-0-06-245307-5 (trade bdg.)

Typography by Brad Mead
17  18  19  20  21   PC/LSCH   10 9 8 7 6 5 4 3 2 1
❖

First Edition

For Donna

# ACKNOWLEDGMENTS

**I stole some names for this book, so now I need to thank** some people. Thank you to Shelbyville High School's Young Writers' Camp students Clare Scudder and Abby Neeb, for allowing me to steal (then twist) their nicknames for Dylan & Arden's World of Warcraft characters. Thank you to Twitter friend Shawntelle Madison for lending me her amazing name and letting me kill the character, too. Many thanks to Allison Trochessett, who had such a pretty last name that my best friend told me about it, thereby forcing me to steal it.

I also stole some shared history. TYVM to my WoW guilds, Riders of Malkier, and The Lambchop Rejects— and especially to Sneakymaa, Whimmy, Farrin, Zamus, Fadain, Amadeous, BabyHuey, Matthea, Aegeous, Chilidog, Pyreah, Moonadrelle,

Scythelord, Punky, and Sheya for ten years of good times. Go Horde or go home!

I didn't steal anything from my deliriously wonderful agent Jim McCarthy, or my tremendously brilliant editor Kristen Pettit—but I would if they asked me to. So many thanks to them for going on this road trip with me, over and over, for years now. I hope it was as special to them as it was to me.

And finally, all the thanks in the world to my wife, Jayne, and my best friend, Wendi. I hope we always drive it like we stole it.

# (2795.70)

**I don't believe in bucket lists. You can't experience a** whole life in fast forward. If somebody told you to eat the best chocolate cake ever in twelve seconds, you wouldn't even taste it.

That's why I never applied to the Wish Foundation people.

For a little kid, a trip to Disneyland is as big as it gets. But they don't know what they're going to miss. They have no idea how big the world is.

I do.

Better now than ever, I do, and this is something else I know: the entryway to the high school doesn't want me. It's pocked up, beaten up—doesn't say hello. The name carved in the limestone isn't even the building's real name anymore. (Melvin Pfeiffer School, it says, in old-fashioned script, like on bibles.)

The sticker on the glass, though—it says Laurel High School, and that's what it is now. I ring the buzzer. Then I wait, a hundred years or something, until a woman's voice crackles, "Can I help you?"

I lean in. I think there's a camera on this thing; I don't know if she needs to see me or what. My voice breaks. "I'm supposed to register today?"

The doors click. That's the answer; I let myself in fast, like there's a countdown or something. When I walk, the bottle of pills in my bag rattles so loud that my heart pounds to cover up the sound.

People are looking at me. There's all kinds of baby-fat cheeks going on here. All kinds of soft and round, bright little eyes, clean little hoodies, and fit skinny jeans.

I try to make myself smaller as I head for the office. I dunno how many of these kids are sophomores, but I'm older than them, I can tell. I'm an alien up in here. Or a wolf with clicky-clicky claws on the waxed floors. A winter wolf, starved and dangerous. I'm too thin; my chest is sort of caved in. If these round, fat babies looked close, they'd see the scars that trace my scalp; they're pearl white under wiry brown hair.

I don't belong here; everything smells like blood.

When I find the office, there's a line. Late slips or some shit; some girl has a *killer* headache and wants to call her mom. It's not even funny, but I'm trying not to laugh at her. She's all neat and tidy, buttoned up and pressed—it's like she came out a factory, out of a box with a plastic window. Her life's so easy, she wants to call mommy instead of grabbing a couple Advil from the nurse.

I almost, I almost want to ask her if she wants an oxy; I got a hundred of 'em in my bag. That's what Medicaid gives you when you have a real killer headache, one that don't respond to chemo or radiation. All that, I could say it, but instead, I stare at the patterns in the carpet until it's my turn.

Fact is, I'm not supposed to have that bottle on me. One, I'm not supposed to be taking them anymore, and more important for two, pretty sure there are *rules* at school about students carrying drugs. There used to be.

"Can I help you?" the receptionist asks. It's almost three, so she looks like she's ready to slap somebody. Since I don't want to be slapped, I keep my distance.

"I'm Dylan Stefansky," I say. When she just stares, I explain some more. "I'm just off hospital leave. I'm supposed to reregister."

The receptionist turns, left, right, searching for something. She plucks up a folder full of papers and starts to hold them out to me. Then her gaze sharpens. Looking past me, she frowns. "Is anyone here with you? A parent or guardian?"

I flatten my lips. That's a sore subject right there. "It's just me and my mom, but I can do the paperwork."

"I'm sure you can," the receptionist says. Straightening up, she holds the folder against her chest. "But I can't register you without a parent or guardian."

My throat tightens. "She works nights; she's sleeping."

Is that sympathy in the receptionist's eyes? Is it pity? I'm sick of both of them, but they're better than watching her lights turn off inside. She doesn't care about me or my mom sleeping off her late shift; all she cares about is rules. "Perhaps she can take a day off. Or rearrange her schedule. I can't register you without a parent or a guardian."

Rage is easy. It flies in first, bloody and ready. It wants me to kick the desk. Fling everything off of it: the late slip box, the sign-in sheet, the little plastic sunflower with sunglasses that bobs its head at me like it's stupid. My face is hot and my hands tremble, but I just stand there. I force myself to stand there and say, real calm, "She can't miss work, though."

The receptionist doesn't sigh. She just shakes her head. "I can give you the paperwork to take home and fill out, but I can't register you without a parent or guardian, Dylan."

"I went here before!" I lean closer. Maybe I even beg a little; I hate myself doing it, but I beg a little. "Please. You can check the computer. I'm in there."

For her, the conversation's over. Instead of telling me to fuck off, she says, "I'm sorry."

Then she holds out the folder. Like a peace offering or something. She's not sorry. She's not sorry one little bit. I turn sharp and hard, and blow out of the office at top speed. Fuck the folder. Fuck her. Fuck this school.

The halls emptied out when I was in the office, so nobody sees me stalk up to the front doors and slam into them hard as I can. Nobody watches when I cut down the stairs, to the car I left parked out front in the bus zone. I wasn't gonna be in there that long, that's what I figured. Guess I didn't realize it was gonna be less than five minutes.

All over, I'm shaking, but I get the keys in the ignition. It's an old-ass car; it doesn't even peel out when I slam my foot down on the gas. It lurches, like the transmission had to stop and google what to do. When the gear finally catches, I sail out of the parking lot.

I'm not going home. For once in my life, I'm not going to the hospital. Somehow, I end up hitting an on ramp. My sludgy transmission finally gets into the spirit and opens up. The car stops rumbling, all the sound but the wind. Baltimore falls away.

Before I know it, I'm forty-seven miles from home. Forty-eight. Forty-nine.

Fifty. I'm not looking back.

And no.

I have no idea where I'm going.

# (NORTHWEST)

**Because she keeps the phone we get because of my**
Medicaid, my mother's not gonna get the chance to flip out on
me, personally. No. My mother's gonna call the cops to report
her car stolen. I can hear her already. No, I can see it, perfectly,
in my head.

Furious, her anger fills up the front yard.

It's generous, calling it a yard. What it *is* is a four-by-four patch
of grass in front of our apartment. But my mother stands in it,
bare feet, bathed in blue and red light. She waves her hands and
points in the wrong direction.

She always points in the wrong direction.

When she says, "Dylan, go run up and get me a Coke," she points at the back of the apartment. Sort of southish. The gas station is northwest, so she's almost exactly wrong. If she wants me to run up to the store and get orange juice, she points west. If I'm supposed to run up to the pharmacy and get my medicine, east.

All of these stores are northwest. There's only one way out of Village Estates. Well two, if you're being morbid. But hey, I got *my* miracle. I'm not allowed to be morbid anymore, fuck you very much.

I'm also not allowed to head due west in a stolen car. A car that my mother's reporting to the police probably right this second. But oh well. She'll cry, because she's good at crying when it gets her something. When it doesn't, she's a bone—dry and cracked. Dusty.

You can tell a lot from the marks on a bone, and you can tell a lot about my mother from the lines on her face.

She's not that old, but there's a fine network between her brows. A map of her life, written in old sunburns and new wrinkles. She wears too much mascara because she says the boys—her brothers, her son—got the pretty eyes in the family. Those lashes fleck when she blinks.

By nightfall, she wears a stippled tattoo on her cheeks. It's a snake, always a snake, riding the deep basin under each eye. According to her, men don't like women who don't take care of themselves. Men don't like eyelashes unless they're thick and crusted with paint. She never asks me what I think; to her I'm not a man. *She* has the answers.

This is all the gospel truth, she says, but she says a lot of things that aren't true.

The first one was that she loved me.

# (EVERYTHING IS RELATIVE)

**Here's something that's true: you can cut the mold off** the cheese and still eat it. It won't kill you.

The government used to hand out cheese, according to my mother. But it was knockoff Velveeta and that's shitty cheese to begin with. American cheese is just plastic that melts, but I like it, grilled up on white bread, the soft, pillowy kind. Not the store brand. That bread's half cardboard shavings, my mother says.

I think there are signs of being rich and being poor, and when we had white Wonder Bread, it meant we weren't poor. It meant mom got better tips than usual. Or she worked more hours. Or somebody gave us a donation, and that meant good bread and actual Coca-Cola. Generic soda's okay, but there's something off about it. Like the bubbles whisper on your tongue, *Tried and couldn't. Almost, but not quite.*

Generic is okay, for some things. For example, real Kraft macaroni and cheese is too . . . something. Too orange? Too big? It fills up my mouth the wrong way and I don't like it. But the store brand is just right.

Suddenly, I laugh. A thin, desperate wheeze that hurts. It digs into my ribs and inflates my head until it could pop. My hands slip on the wheel and the car swerves. Anxiety squashes the laughter, and I hurry to steer straight. Bad enough I stole this car. If I wreck it, that'll be the living end. *The living goddamned end*, my mother would say.

But what am I even thinking? Cheap mac and cheese? When's the last time I ate anything and thought it was good?

Radiation and chemo do that to you. Burn out whatever it is you taste with, leave you with a bitter metal tongue all the time. Mashed potatoes. Watermelon. It's all like sucking on a dirty fountain penny.

I'm all better now (Miracle, bitches!) but a Big Mac still tastes like shit.

Right about now, I *want* a Coke and some cold fried chicken, and some peanut butter mashed up with bananas, and fried onions and green peppers, and probably some pickled onions and cucumbers. I want them only because I remember them— what they were. And what they were was *good*.

My face gets hot, and that means I'm going to cry and that pisses me off more than anything. My bone-dry mother has a whole waterfall waiting to spill, whenever she wants something. Those tears fall when she *wants* them to. Me, I cry over a dinner I can't have, and don't have, and that wouldn't taste good even if I got it.

I cry about everything. The wrong song on the radio. A tag left in my t-shirt to itch me. My neighbor turning off their Wi-Fi because I stole too much of it today. The book I got that didn't end the way I wanted it to. Cry, cry, cry. I'm salt-soaked probably seventy percent of the time.

For a while there, it was all right. Mostly all right. You're supposed to cry in the beginning, when they tell you that you're gonna die. When you *come to terms*.

But then, get with the program, damn it. Be strong. Be a role model. March off to chemo like a soldier and don't stop until you beat that shit.

I was a bad patient, because I cried at the clinic.

Behind the desk there, there were school pictures from their patients. One of the biggest ones was Shawntelle Grace. Everything about her was perfect; when all her hair fell out, her head was smooth and round. She stayed beautiful, even I could see that. Black skin and brown eyes, and that smile. Damn, that smile.

*She* didn't cry; she kept on smiling the whole time she was sick. The ward scrapbook was full of articles about her; they all start with some variation of *you wouldn't know by looking at her, but Shawntelle Grace is fighting for her life.*

Then it goes on: *here's Shawntelle running her school's food drive at Thanksgiving. Here's Shawntelle reading to a brain-damaged puppy. Here's Shawntelle, walking on water.*

The last one is *here's Shawntelle's pink granite gravestone with a Mother Teresa quote on it* and pictures of the funeral procession. What a role model. That's how you're supposed to die, all dignified and meaningful. There's *rules*. There's a *playbook*. You're not supposed to go out clutching and sobbing and scared.

To get a story in the newspaper, you're supposed to be cheerful every single day. Strong and brave and unafraid—a *fighter*.

No staring at your ceiling at night, no panic attacks that turn everything slow motion. Definitely no sour sweat and puke on your skin and hiding in the dark because it hurts when you breathe.

No. You need to be inspirational, so it's *sad* when you *lose this battle*.

They're never gonna write that story about me. I mean, they can't now, anyway. I got better. Shocked everybody. They called it spontaneous remission and acted like it was touch-and-go, but even I knew the tumor was gone. No more *killer* headaches. I stopped falling over my own feet. I saw straight, I remembered shit.

*I got better.*

But I still wasn't the good patient. Because then, because then I was supposed to jump back in, like the last couple years didn't even happen. They gave me a sheet of paper and said, "You don't need those narcotics anymore, you stick to this schedule."

See, they don't care if you're a junkie if you're gonna die. But once you're sticking around, no more barrel-sized bottles of drugs for *you*.

I didn't detox right, either. Because here's the thing—they were sure I was gonna die. *I* was sure. People stopped talking about the next round of treatment and started talking about palliative care, and you know what that is? They dose you up good so you don't know you're dying. More drugs. Not less.

So then, we get the scans that came back blank, and holy shit. I'm all better. Even with the touch-and-go dance they did, they started talking follow-ups and five-year-out percentages and, yeah, detox. Practically overnight, they go from *let's give this sad fuck all the morphine in the world* to *no more drugs for you.* What I got was a nurse who explained how I was supposed to taper down, eight pills for seven days, then six pills, down and around until no more pills at all.

So I half-dosed myself out. Yeah, I did, because they were *sure* I was dying, then they were *sure* I wasn't, and you know what I was sure of? Being that sick and in that much pain was agony. If it can go away like magic, it can come back like magic, too. I didn't want to be left hanging if (when) it did.

Every time I was supposed to take two, I took one. Every time I was supposed to take one, I took half, and it was hell. The itches, the shakes, the hallucinations, all that shit—I puked almost as much coming off the drugs as I did during chemo. But I did it, and in the end, I had one bottle left. One hundred tablets. A hundred more than I was supposed to have.

Detox shoulda left me with nothing. But like I said, I was a bad patient. I complained about cold hands, needles, drugs, the nurse's garlic breath, the orderly that banged my gurney against the corner, chemo, not getting chemo, my hair falling out, my hair coming back in wiry, the d.t.'s, the shakes, the rebound headaches. Nobody was writing the inspirational story about my shit, because I wasn't doing it right, was I?

Yeah, well, you know what? I *was* fighting. Just not the way they wanted me to.

Now I'm running. And I'm not doing that right either, because I still don't know where I'm going.

# (MEET IN THE MIDDLE)

**The way I figure it, if something's bad, go ahead and** make it worse. Got in trouble for stealing somebody's lunch out of the coat room? Go ahead and kick the principal, too. Blew off the first day of the rest of your life? Steal your mom's car, while you're at it.

And even if you're starting to fall asleep a little, keep going. Keep driving.

The road blurs, and I veer. Rumble strips on the shoulder buzz. The sound wraps around my throat, squeezing me until I can't breathe. The water I'm under is mine. Humid, salt, all up in my head. Filling up my lungs. Everything stretches out of reach, out of control.

With shaking hands, I jerk the wheel. Off the highway, onto the shoulder. For one brilliant, time-stopped second, it looks like I'm going to skid into the ditch. I stomp the brakes and yelp when the back end fishtails. But then it stops; everything stops.

I throw it into Park and collapse. Raw, ugly sobs tear at my throat. They come out like animal sounds, rough and wild. The air conditioner keens, too. There's something stuck down in the system, whistling away.

Tepid air dribbles out, hardly cold. My breath fills up the car, ragged but slowing. I drag a hand across my eyes, then blink and my sight clears. Emotion drains away, and all that's left is the uneven buzz in the engine, and an uneven ache beneath my skin.

Cars fly by. I feel them; their wake pulls like gravity. It's almost night, and the sky's blossoming with stars.

There are roads going everywhere and nowhere. I used to think that was amazing. How all that pavement was a choose your own adventure. Set off on the right path, and you'd end up in Las Vegas. Or New York. Or anywhere—everywhere was possible on the right road.

One of them—this one I'm currently on—leads, eventually, to

the Salton Sea. A body of water trapped in the middle of a desert, full of salt and pesticides and algae—dead fish wash up on the shore. It wasn't always that way. There's a resort out there from the fifties, all crusted and rusted and decaying, too. They pumped that thing full of chemicals and killed it.

They pumped chemicals into me and saved my life.

Now that I think about it, we're sitting at the crossroads of the alive/dead highway, huh? We belong together, me and the Salton Sea. At least for a minute. Long enough to shake hands.

A semi blasts by. My heart pounds, the Monte Carlo shakes, and I realize how fucking stupid it would be to die in a car crash on the side of the road after surviving brain cancer. Everything pops into focus; I have to get my shit together.

Digging around, I produce a handful of McDonald's napkins. I scrub my face with them, and inhale the scent of historical french fries. A different ache rolls through my belly, and fine. I'll go eat something. Even though it will suck.

I have to roll the window down to see if it's clear—the side mirror is long gone. I wonder where it is. Junkyard? Dump? Maybe some kid picked it up and took it home. It could be reflecting anything right now. The shape of a girl learning to play the guitar. Some stoner discovering his fingers at the edge of the universe. Maybe the sea; maybe the sky.

Like a dog, I lean all the way out the window and breathe. I smell oil and gas and grass and in the distance, rain. Nobody coming; it's clear for me to go. I slide back behind the wheel and pull onto the pavement again.

This car will speed, but only if I trade it for a terrifying shake over sixty-five. I buzz and bump with it, and it's like a hive of bees swarming over my skin. They fill my ears and blot out my senses. All I have is my sight, and that's blurry from the vibration.

But it's hard to feel anything else with all this shaking. And I swear, I could sleep like this. I really could.

# (2652.2)

**The green and white sign overhead reads AMARANTH.**

*Amaranth*, why is that familiar? It's one of the exits coming up, and it's stuck in my head. I want to sing it. But I don't even know how to pronounce it. Not out loud.

I know a lot of words like that. I got them out of books. I know what they mean, but I have no idea how to say them. *Bonafide*, now, I'm pretty sure that's bone-a-fied. Somebody at the clinic pronounced it bone-a-fee-dee, but I don't think that's right.

*Chiffonade* is definitely shiff-uh-nod, I figured that one out thanks to the Food Network closed-captioning in the hospital. Roll that basil up and slice it into itty bitty ribbons: chiffonade, bitches.

But Amaranth . . . what is that?

According to the signs, there's gas-food-lodging here, but I'm half-a-tank, not staying. I pull into the gas station right off the highway. It's a good waypoint, someplace I can sit and think. I know Amaranth means *something*. I just can't drag it out of my head yet.

I park in the far end of the lot and the sudden quiet does a number on me. Too quiet. Too almost dark. Suddenly, my brain decides it *needs* something. Needs some noise, or some food, or hey, how about a pill or two or six? I scrabble for the bottle down in my bag.

It takes nothing to open it up, and I stare into it. The pills are packed in good, all the way to the top. They smell like nothing; found out the hard way about a thousand times that they taste like shit on top of bitter metal. I learned to take some water in my mouth, throw the pills in, and swallow fast fast fast.

Except, I don't need them. I don't need them anymore. There's nothing in my head but brains. Nothing in my lungs but air. All I am is tired, and fucked up, and the pills are familiar. I fish one out and rub it between my fingers; it leaves a white trace of powder on my skin. Then, I throw it out the window and slump behind the wheel.

My bones are jelly; my skin is goo. I could seep into the seats and be another stain for my mother to bitch about.

# (MY MOTHER)

**He's been a pain in my ass since the day he was born,** I imagine my mom saying as she reports the stolen vehicle. I've heard her say it before. Usually to Lynne, a yes-man if ever there was one.

*Mmm-hmm,* Lynne hums soothingly, as though my pain-in-the-assery is a foregone conclusion.

Right now, I'm costing my mother money. How is she gonna get to work? But Lynne will pick her up. Lynne is my mother's very own hallelujah chorus.

*—If I got cancer, I'd just have to die of it.*

*—Mmm-hmm.*

*—It's not like Medicaid covers everything.*

*—Lord, I know, Becky.*

*—If it did, would I have to work this hard?*

*—No, baby. Of course not.*

*—That's all I do. I work and I work and it all goes right back out the door. Don't I deserve something?*

*—Hell yes. Treat yourself. What's ten dollars?*

Thanks, Lynne. Thanks for being there when my mother was inconvenienced because I was dying. Thanks for helping spend what little money we do have.

But then, Lynne's entitled to a say, I guess.

A couple summers ago, Lynne had the bright idea of pasting my picture on a bunch of empty tin cans. Talked people at the gas station and the market and all the stores up and down the state road to put them by the registers. LITTLE DYLAN NEEDS CHEMOTHERAPY PLEASE HELP GOD BLESS.

A couple summers ago, I was fourteen and awkward and bald and covered in sores. Had my first knotty scar looping over my ear; my skin was grey tissue paper. Nobody gives money (or rings) to Gollum, so they used a picture from my seventh birthday instead.

Back then, I was brown eyed and bright faced and making all kinds of smiles over the new-used bike I got after I blew out my candles. That ride was choice. It had streamers on the handlebars, and slightly faded stars on the seat, and it was mine all mine.

Little Dylan *did* need chemotherapy. That part wasn't a lie. Little Dylan got it, too, paid for by the state. Change and crumpled ones in stewed tomato cans, that was *fun money*. My mother and Lynne got cigarettes. Fingernail polish with glitter suspended in it. A trip to a casino or six, lots of off-track betting slips because a horse named Everly's Golden Sunshine couldn't lose. (Spoiler alert—yes, it could.)

For a while there, we always had Coca-Cola and Wonder Bread. I won't lie to you. I bought twenty-two books, barely used. A soft comforter for my bed. A subscription to World of Warcraft. Even though my laptop's so slow that I have to play it with all the special effects turned off, I love WoW.

Yes, there's something I love.

No, it's not real, but so what?

Clapping my hands to the wheel, I suddenly realize why I'm in Amaranth. World of Warcraft.

Arden.

Arden's here.

I have to find her.

# (SEVEN DAYS FROM THE SALTON SEA)

**We're gonna go on a quest, me and her. A real-life quest,** and there's gonna be dragons and roads untaken and who knows all what, but it's gonna be real. I deserve it; I let the Wish people pass me over, and I shouldn't have. I was all screwed up in my head; what the hell was wrong with them, listening to me when I said no?

Out of the imaginary world and into the real one. One long first walk—well, not walk, or I wouldn't make it to the corner. It's been a long time since this bag of bones did crazy shit like exercise or running or walking; I'm out of breath just thinking about it. But a trip. There's no wishing for wishes now. No more money, no more little Dylan. No more anything, and I've got to escape. I want Arden to come with me; it's dangerous to go alone.

Our quest . . . what's it gonna be?

Not Disneyland. Or the Statue of Liberty. Or the Grand Canyon or a white-sand beach. Those are for the little kids. My thoughts tick and ache. Cogs grind in my brain, off center. Those are ordinary places. They live on maps; where's the magic? Where are the monsters?

Why not Atlantis? There was a flood that washed the rings of the city away, but it seemed to me like, if archaeologists can find shit like dinosaur feathers and Neanderthal footprints, why can't I find a whole city? Probably because we can't drive to the Straits of Gibraltar?

Pick something. Damn it, Dylan, think. Something with magic and lies. Something like the game. Something impossible and possible.

Then, I know. I know what it is, what it always was.

Back in the day, there was this guy, Iturbe or something, he sailed to the New World from Spain, then up and down the California coast. He stole a metric shit-ton of pearls from the

Kumeyaay Indians there, and thought he was gonna get away with it too.

Except back then, those Spanish bitches thought that California was an island. What Iturbe sailed up was the Colorado River, all flooded because of hard rain.

But not that deep—he got almost to the Salton Sea when he ran aground. Had to leave that ship full of stolen pearls and limp on home by way of Mexico. He sent people back to find his pearl ship, but they never did. Earthquakes and sand and time swallowed it up. Iturbe died poor as shit, which is about as fair as it gets, if you ask me.

Anyway, people have been looking for his ship ever since, a ghost galleon in the Mojave Desert.

Yes. That's exactly right. My head swims; for a second I lose the thread. Strings of pearls roll away as I try to focus. It was always this place. It was always that crossroads; it makes sense now. Maybe I didn't *realize* I had started a quest when I got turned out of the school, but I had. Picked it right up and providence put me on the right path.

I didn't have to believe in destiny to let it guide me.

# (JUMP ON YOUR TOON;
## LET'S GO)

**Okay, I got World of Warcraft because when I was on** chemo, then radiation, then most of the way to dying, with sores and nutrition shakes (which are not shakes; shakes are cold and creamy and they don't taste like vitamin dust), I wasn't supposed to go outside.

I couldn't leave and I needed to, so bad. So I bitched and cried and yelled and made my mother almost as miserable as me. That's why she let me spend almost a hundred dollars out of the donation cans to get a video game. Anything to shut me up so she could get back to how all this affected *her*.

Warcraft was exactly what I wanted. I read faster than the

bookmobile could bring me new books, but the game had stories that went on for what seemed like ever.

We only had to pay for the subscription. Our neighbor's Wi-Fi was practically begging me to use it. No password, and the hub or the station or whatever it's called was named ShareMe. So I did. And I logged into a whole other world.

Most of the time, people think video games are just for shooting stuff. But there's a story in Azeroth—that's the name of the land you play in, in Warcraft.

And not just by yourself, there's people. Tons of people. They're all logging in, all around the world, all at the same time. While I'm walking around as my Shaman (I can heal, I can fight, I can bring back the dead. It doesn't mean anything; don't read anything into it.), millions of other people are walking around, too. You pick a race, like Orc or Goblin, and you pick a job, like Warrior or Mage, and then you get thrown into a whole new world.

The world looks real. Yeah, there's magic and stuff, but a mountain is a mountain. Trees are trees. If you're around at sunset, you can watch the sun go down. Throw a fishing line in some water and it makes ripples. Boats come and go. You can take a walk through the forest. You can ride beasts and hot air balloons and trains.

If you decide to take a swim, you can go to the shore. There's nobody telling you that you can't go in. Dive under and the water gets so deep, it goes down and down, into murky, ghostly places. If you don't come up for air, you drown. It's scary to get too far below the waves, when it starts to get dark and your life is running out.

There's quests to do, and places to visit. There are cities and fairs and festivals. Me and Arden finally did the Midsummer Fire Festival quests last year. She got a glowing crown and a gold dress. All she had to do was click on it, and it threw fire in the air and made her dance. She sparked and blazed, crazy beautiful.

Arden wasn't the only one goofing off. I have a bunch of shape-shifting toys. She danced, and I turned myself into a blue, hissing snake-dude. Then I froze myself in amber. Then I turned myself into a Dwarf made of iron. Right on the steps of the auction house, we danced and changed and changed and danced.

When Arden's in her regular shape, she waves her arms in the air, a slow, snakey goth dance. I do the Electric Slide—it's programmed in, those are the only steps we can do. You have to be one of the pretty races to get something sexy. But she plays a Forsaken, a rotting zombie chick, and I play a Tauren—a black-and-white cow-chick. We don't do sexy.

I've been playing with her almost every day for three years. We've walked, her Forsaken, my Tauren, from Winterspring to Uldum, and that means nothing to you. But trust me, it's a long way. It's like walking from New York City to Miami. We swam up the coast once, from Tanaris to Azshara—San Diego to Seattle, sort of. For no reason. We could have caught a flight or ridden our mounts. But we went because we could. To see what would happen if we did.

Dungeon crawling and finding ancient artifacts, and sometimes just sitting on top of the world and talking. Typing, anyway.

I've never heard her voice. She wanted to chat real-time; and she kept pushing for me to turn on the voice chat in the game, or get Ventrilo—it does the same thing. It runs on the computer, letting everybody on the game talk for real. One touch of a button and it would be like a phone call, right in each other's ears. Arden's voice in my brain and mine in hers. But the donation money had run out. No way was my mother gonna shell out for a headset.

Anyway, why bring real life into it? Inside the game, I could do stuff I couldn't in this stupid, wasted body. I wasn't some sad, dying gay kid who got short of breath walking to the bathroom. She wasn't a trans girl trying to get her dad to just be chill. In Azeroth, we could be whoever we wanted.

Inside the game, I was alive and confident, strong and funny, and Arden was sweet and excitable and up for anything. I could make a fifteen-minute flight from one end of Kalimdor to the other for *fun*. When our toons were little, Arden knew all the paths and shortcuts so we could even make the trip by land, if we wanted to. (Now she can turn into a Sandstone Drake, and I just ride on her back to wherever we want to go.)

The point always was, it was us. Together. Free. I flirted with her; she flirted with me. And why not? Why shouldn't we? Whatever we did, it didn't change us or the game.

It didn't even matter if we died there. Our bodies were always right where our souls left them.

All we had to do was run back and start again.

# (REAL ID)

**I wind myself up to walk inside the gas station. All I have** to say is that I have a flat and my phone is dead and look at him hard. I'm ashy and gaunt; my hair is wiry, wavy, sticking all out because I can't keep my hands out of it. I'm probably fucking terrifying at this point—maybe that'll work in my favor.

The dude doesn't blink. He just hands his phone over and goes back to sorting cigarettes.

Now I have leftover adrenaline, but that's okay. I still have to move fast. I do something I've never done before: I log into the website for my Warcraft account and turn on Real ID. For some reason, this game company thinks people who run around pretending to be goblins and dwarves want people in real life to be able to find them.

Maybe they're right. Arden's had it on for a while now. Adding me as soon as she got it, she waited for a tag back. A long time, too. Now I'm finally doing it, and I feel like I'm about to choke on my own tongue.

It worked; it worked. As soon as my account refreshes, I have exactly what I came for. Takes all of two seconds, and I have Arden's real name.

D. Arden Trochessett.

I cradle the phone and frown. Arden's easy, but my mouth won't wrap around that last name. I don't know where to start pronouncing it. Too many T's and S's laying side by side. So what? I can't pronounce it, but it's exactly the kind of name I need. Rare. Unusual.

I type *Trochessett* and *411* into the search engine. Up pops one phone number in all of Amaranth that matches. Right next to it, one address. That goes into the clerk's map app, and a red line leads me straight to Arden's front door. Borrowing the credit-card pen, I draw it on the inside of my wrist.

"Thanks," I tell the guy, returning his phone. I don't want to steal it. It's nice, but so's the clerk.

"Somebody coming to help you?"

"Sort of," I say. I buy a bottle of water, 'cause I think I'm gonna need it, and then I get my head on straight. As I walk out to the car, I study the map on my wrist. It's not too complicated, but I didn't pay attention. That one long line could be two blocks or five miles. What the hell, though. Why not?

I throw open the car and grab my bag. I don't have much. Gum, pens, dumb shit. My bottle of pills. The Tic Tacs in the glove box. A foil space blanket with a tear in it—I go ahead and take that, and I don't know why. Because it's there, I guess, and I don't want to walk away with nothing.

That car smells like stale grease, old shoes. It smells like the decrepit stuffing in the backseat, green and grainy and old. To hell with that car. Let the police tow it back home. Now it's not stolen and now nobody can find me. That's better than knowing nobody wants to.

Anyway, that's where this quest starts—with me walking away from my mother's car. It's on the edge of dark, and I have a half-ass map, but I don't care. It's not like a quest is supposed to be easy. If you can just walk through it, who gives a shit, right? You gotta work for it; you gotta bleed for it. So I take a swallow of cold, tinny water, and start down the street.

The drive into Amaranth made it look like one of the villages in the game. Red roofs and pretty trees. A cathedral lining up the horizon just so. But on the ground, it's real obvious I'm not in Elwynn Forest. Real life Amaranth looks like real-life anywhere. The strip I'm on is kinda industrial, but it gives way to neighborhoods after a while.

Now Amaranth is anywhere *nice*. The houses have neat front yards. Trees stretch up and out. Some of the sidewalk squares are crooked, but that's only because the roots pushed them up.

People put their names on the mailboxes. And flags, too. Flowers climb up the posts, their blossoms watching you approach. Like they want to say hello or something. At home, I have a rusted pocket nailed to the outside wall. Right by the door. The numbers peeled off a long time ago.

Amaranth is quiet. Cars come and go, mostly at the speed limit. Nobody sits on their porches or yells out the windows. Pills rattle in my bag, and I clutch it to my chest. This place makes me nervous, like the whole town might be coiled up. Waiting. Windows glow, houses probably full of blue-eyed freaks.

What if that's what's waiting in Arden's house? What if her stepmom opens the door, wearing a silk scarf and sharp-lined lipstick? Her tiny little nostrils will clamp shut when she smells the cheap on me. She probably won't even know who I am.

And even though I've been talking to her for years, I suddenly realize *Arden* don't know who I am, either, not exactly. We met in the game. A game where she calls me Sutterglut, or Sutty for short, and sometimes if it's been a real long night and we're punchy, Moo Moo Kitty.

Who uses their real name in the game? I mean, shit, can you imagine? Like, you walk up to the dungeon in Karazhan, who's gonna believe it was owned by an ancient, evil Arch-Mage named Jerome Brown? You don't journey to the belly of a lava dungeon in search of Brad Stertz.

What am I thinking? What exactly am I hoping to accomplish here?

It doesn't matter. Sucking up deep, humid breaths that taste like the slowly approaching rain, I make myself walk. No more thinking. Just one foot in front of the other. My spine rattles. My head hurts.

According to the scans, according to everybody, even according to me, I know it's just a headache, a regular one. People get them, it happens. But my pills rattle in my bag, and they remind me. Maybe not. Maybe it all comes back—one more step and it's back to seizureland for me.

That's how a lot of kids find out they have cancer, actually.

Start out with a headache, get clumsy, flop around like a fish on a dock, go directly to dead.

The osteo kids, I think maybe they have it worse. They go for a jump shot, come down and break a leg. Tough titty for the starting center with a scholarship to Stanford. You're going somewhere else, my friend. There's no scholarship, and you're never coming home.

A lot of us get better. Most of us, actually. You roll up on a kids' cancer ward and you get a lot of leukemia, a lot of brainies like me, a lot of Hodgkin's. We go through hell and we get better; that's just the way it is.

Most of us don't get to end-stage and turn around at the last minute, though. So me? I'm still waiting for it to come back.

I'm not ready, but I'm prepared, and maybe I should take something when I get to where I'm going . . .

All that thinking, and somehow, I got to where I was going.

Arden's house is blue and white, and the downstairs windows are dark.

# (SILVER)

**I stand in the shadows and hate the front door.**

It's white. Fresh, clean, brand-new white with a door knocker that looks like a ring of ivy. It's heavy, with all kinds of shades and shadow in it. It's so perfect it nearly looks real.

Who pays for something like that? How much did it cost? I hate that I always wonder that, but I want to know. I think it says a lot about somebody—how they spend extra money.

It costs me seventy-seven bucks (and ninety-four cents) a year to play World of Warcraft, but I *need* that. Fighting and screaming, I made my mother give me that. Lynne says my disability should pay for it, but what does she know?

I pick up the ivy door knocker and let it drop. It's a dare. If nobody hears it, I'll just go home. Quest: failed. Though I want to, I don't press my head against the wood. Wrapping my arms around myself, I shiver and wait.

This is stupid. There's not an undead rogue waiting for me inside this house. There's no such thing as an undead rogue, anyway; it's all pixels and lies.

*No, you stole a car and came here,* an annoying part of my brain argues. *It's real. Arden is, anyway.*

I should run. But when I look down I realize—my legs aren't interested or able. I'm in remission, but I'm not well.

So I'm still standing there when a human being answers the door.

This man is a stranger. Grey hair, grey eyes, and pajamas like people wear on TV. Matching top and bottoms. He's old, and suddenly I'm praying. *Don't make me go home. Don't turn me away. I know it's late and I look like shit, but come on, man.*

He looks past me, frowning. Turning, I wanna know what he's looking at, too, but there's nothing to see.

"Can I help you?"

I don't know what to say. He's not mean. He's not nice. He's just *there*, concrete blocks for legs and stones for eyes. I could be a fly on his porch, buzzing and buzzing. Too far away to matter, but too close to ignore entirely.

I haven't uttered a sound, and he's already decided about me. He makes me want to walk on his potato salad.

I have to put my tongue in the right place to say the words. "Arden has my Dragon Age CD."

Concrete Blocks stiffens. "Who?"

For a second, I panic. Did I call her Nuba? In case I did, I clarify. "Arden. Arden has my game; she said I could come by and get it."

For another second, the man stares through me. Then he turns, his flannel jammie pants whispering as he walks to the foot of the stairs. Those are some quality stairs, too. The steps are wood, the rail is carved fancy. That's a staircase for a movie. A staircase to fall down and die on. I wonder what would happen if I grabbed a laundry basket and just slid down that thing in it. Instant roller coaster.

I'm so caught up living the life suggested by that banister that I don't hear the man say anything. When footsteps interrupt my fantasyland, I realize he just walked away. No kidding. Pulled out his phone, tippity-typeity, then turned and went.

If I was a meth-head spree killer, he'd be dead. But I'm not, and the door is still open.

My heart beats hard. It skips, and my head goes soft and fuzzy. There are feet on the stairs, attached to silver-patterned leggings. They disappear under a soft silver tunic, one that stretches across broad shoulders, and my brain just stops. It stops.

As long as I've known Arden, my mental picture of her has been digital. She has purple hair and glowing yellow eyes; she's a zombie in leather armor. When I see Arden on a regular day, she says hello with two daggers that are longer than the exposed bones of her arms.

But Arden in real life doesn't match my memories.

She's not Forsaken, first of all. Second of all, even though I know her, and I know who she is, I can't help seeing the body she was born with, even in her leggings and tunic. Broad shoulders and narrow hips, green eyes squinting curiously at me beneath dark, shaped brows. Her face is soft; it resolves into a strong jawline and a pretty neck. I feel like an asshole for reacting to her body; I feel like I should do this better.

But who wouldn't look at Arden twice? Who wouldn't stand there and stare at somebody beautiful like that? Jesus, I've got a knot in my chest and I can't catch a breath. She's burned in, like an image after the flash, making my blood run fast and hot.

But that's flesh and I've got a brain. Forcing myself to breathe, I twist my thoughts back into shape. I'm gay, she's a girl—these things are just true.

"I'm sorry," Arden says, and it sounds like she means it. "Do I know you?"

My mouth tastes like bitter metal on old leather. I have Yoda on my tongue, my voice comes out creaky and wrong. "You don't recognize me?"

It's not a game. She's not an undead rogue, and I'm not a magic cow. We're just people, standing here on a porch in the dark. Just a couple of feet, and miles and miles away from each other.

Tears spring up, but I force them back.

I might have considered crying in front of Nuba. But this is D.

Arden LastnameIcan'tpronounce. A stranger. I shake my head and it hurts—not just my head. Everything—my chest, the way it seizes, and my thoughts, too. This isn't what I wanted.

Humiliation laced with depression: it's a hell of a drug.

It's just, I want her to recognize me. This one thing, I want it to be real. Us. This life, that life in the game, that time we spent together. I need it to be real. God, need it so bad that my insides bubble and roil.

Arden clutches the frame of the door with one hand, but she steps out. Anchored. Safe, because she's out, but still in at the same time. Something flickers across her face, hesitation maybe? But all the same she leans toward me and murmurs, "Dylan?"

Catching the porch rail so I don't fall. I'm tired and my head's killing me. But she knows my name, she does. She knows *me*. Everything whites out for a second. I'm dreaming on my feet, flying away.

Probably because I don't answer right away, Arden lowers her voice even more. "Sutty?"

My name in the game. How I first met her. It just tripped off her tongue. Everything breaks inside; emotions rush out, they spill out of me. I'm drowning under a wave. Now I have to cry, because I'm real, and she's real, and we're standing on the same front porch, under the same constellations, in the same world. I can't stay on my feet anymore, so I sit down hard and nod.

"Yeah. Yeah it is, Arden. It's me."

She drops and hugs me tight, for a second. For a flash. Then almost as fast, she backs off. It was like touching me was burning her. There were too many possible reasons why, but all I knew was that for one second, everything was perfect—and then it was gone.

Arden invites me inside and I can't even look at her. Words and worries spin around in my head. I'm not her memories of me, either. In the game, if I said, *let's go on a quest, let's go on an adventure*, she would say yes. Done deal. Easy.

What's she going to say when it's just me?

# (THiS IS HOW i MEET THE ONLY FRiEND I HAVE LEFT)

**Arden walks me upstairs and locks the door behind us.**
Leaning her forehead against the wood, she seems overwhelmed.

Her back arches, one shoulder blade higher than the other. Her fingers curl on the knob. Motion washes through her; she's the sea, drawing away from the shore. "You want to hear something crazy?" she asks.

"Always," I reply.

She exhales a long breath. "I was afraid something had happened. When the Real ID popped up, I was afraid your mom was logging in to tell me you were dead."

I drift through Arden's physical space and settle on her bed. It smells spicy, with an edge of dark to it. It's hard to settle into her scent, because it stirs me up. I feel like I'm stealing something, cutting glances at her when she can't see. But look at her. She's made out of hearts; she has stars in her eyes.

I drop my bag on my feet. That bright spark of pain is distracting, and good, because now I can say something. "My mother doesn't know about you."

"Oh," she says. She looks hurt.

I spread my hands on the sheets, her sheets. "She doesn't know the difference between Warcraft and Minecraft. I doubt she realizes I even play anymore."

This time, when she says, "Oh," it's softer.

She slides off the door, her body gliding easily. When she moves, it's smooth. Dancing from step to step, a bloom of arms and legs, she comes to sit beside me. Not too close. She puts a whole body length between us. I'm disappointed and grateful. I don't wanna like her for the wrong reasons, and I'm afraid all my reasons are wrong.

It's weird to sit in her room. To see her real face and her real skin. I don't know how to talk to Arden outside the game. I'm used to sitting with Nuba, and she's somewhere in Azeroth, too far away for me to reach.

There's an echo when I pluck at the sheets. My hands feel detached. I don't like it, part of my body checking out on me. What if it means something bad? I haven't been not-sick long enough to believe it's gonna stick, you know? But probably I'm just tired. I've been going awhile. I need to pass out, but I can't do that, can I? I just got here.

Uneasy, I rock forward, then back. Instead of looking at her, I look at her toes. Her bare toes, square little toes, every one perfectly straight. Each nail painted, but a different color. A rainbow when she walks.

Finally, I say, "I can leave."

"Are you crazy?"

"Maybe." I lean back, my thin hair crunching against the wall. "I just rolled up on you, no notice. You weren't expecting me."

Slipping beside me, Arden wraps herself up in her arms and studies my face. "Yeah, I was. I mean, online, but this is better, right?"

It's sweet that she says that. Maybe she even means it. Looking around, I'm pretty sure it really would be the second worst thing in her world if her gaming buddy quit showing up. Oh darn, her day is ruined, her stepmom got the orange juice with the pulp. Wrong color car for her birthday, dang it.

And I'm a dick, even thinking that. Who cares about *stuff* when her dad won't stop calling her *son*?

Does the nice room make it better? No. No, it doesn't, but damn. It's not just nice. It's *rich*.

It's about a thousand times better than my room in Village Estates. Back there, there's barely enough room for a full-sized mattress (and that's my mother's old set). The bed goes almost from wall to wall, lengthwise, underneath my window. The walls are grey. They used to be white because that's the only color we're allowed to paint them, but I like to put my feet on them when I read.

Arden's got a TV as big as a movie poster. Two computers, and a laptop. On her desk, her cell phone is charging, one of those great big ones that can do all the tricks. The air smells good; there's no stains on the ceiling. One wall is this unmarked, pearly blue and the others are sort of silver. She has art with frames, and nothing stuck up with thumbtacks.

It's a showroom, and Arden sits in the middle of it like it's not fucking amazing.

Her skin is smooth and her teeth are straight and all this clean perfection is suddenly driving me crazy. For a long time, I don't say anything. I'm afraid to move, like dirty and poor will flake off me and ruin all this. She's gotta know that, because she steals a look at me from the corner of her eyes. Then her gaze darts away again.

Pulling a foot into her lap, she grinds her thumbs into the arch. When she catches me turned her way, she smiles. Her shoulders curve, like she's folding into herself.

Fear skitters across my skin—a tick, a flea. If Arden looks too long, she'll see everything about me that Warcraft hides. I'm not brave. I'm not strong. I'm not *anything*. No wait, that's not true. I'm an idiot, because I stole a car and I came here thinking I'd waltz in and say, let's go on a quest and she'd say, yeah let's go, I've been waiting for this my whole life.

Mouth dry, I look for something to hold on to. Something to keep it all from spinning away. My gaze falls on her stuff again, and I ask, "You have the game on your laptop?"

"Yeah," she says. Her face clears, an inside light turning on.

"You wanna play?"

Without a thought, she puts her Mac in my hands, and she bounds over to her desk. Pushing crap out of her way, she pulls up Warcraft on that big-ass screen and logs in. I keep stealing looks because I want to see what the game looks like on a monitor like that. Big and beautiful, realer than I've ever seen it.

Turns out her laptop is almost as good. Everything bad shifts back. My headache's starting to fade; my tight chest loosens up some. Meeting Arden is terrifying, but now it's kind of amazing. All of a sudden, I'm seeing our real world, mine and hers, with all the magic turned on. There's so many details that I never saw before.

Last night, we logged out together. And on the screen, there's Arden standing right next to me. We're exactly where we left each other, exactly where we belong.

This is what's normal for us: tinkly music in the background and Goblins wandering by trying to sell us springs and gears. And Arden, in the skin I know best. Purple-haired and half-rotted. Some kind of punk zombie. I'm a cow-Shaman, and right now I feel more like myself than I do in real life.

I type, but I say out loud, too, "Hey, sexy, Where're we going?"

"Darkmoon Faire?" she asks. I hear her relief, even as her words pop up on my screen. Maybe this is what it would have been like if we'd been voice chatting this whole time. Easy to talk, comfortable in real life. "I'm tired of grinding rep."

"Lead the way," I tell her. But before I follow, I cast a healing spell just to see it with the effects turned on. Ribbons of enchanted water swirl around my hands. They explode into silvery fireflies, sparks and stars and shadows I never saw on my old laptop.

Everything's brand-new.

# (KEYSMASH)

**It's easy to burn off hours in a video game. Everything's** beautiful, and nothing hurts for long. Midnight comes and goes. We get bored screwing around at the Faire and end up grinding rep on daily quests.

Basically, we're doing the same quests over and over, earning points to buy better gear. With better gear, we can kill bigger monsters. And why do we want to kill bigger monsters? They drop better gear. This whole game is the sound of one hand clapping.

But we do it because we like it. Because want to *see* the big monsters. And here's the thing—it's just me and Arden; we gotta figure out how to do all this stuff, just the two of us. Even though there's a Looking for Group tool, we don't use it. That way lies madness: aggros who call everything and everybody a fag, griefers who drop connection just to get everybody killed, and fucking n00bs (shitty players) who need to stop QQ and l2p (quit crying and learn to play).

Me and Arden, we're never gonna be in a group big enough to take down the really impressive shit. But we do all right, the two of us.

And right now, we're doing all right, too. Every time Arden types *LOL*, she actually does it. For real, she laughs out loud. Sometimes just low and under her breath, amused. Then, there are times when she throws her head back. Her whole body; she laughs with all of it.

All the flirting we do in the game makes sense in the box, and now, a little bit out of it. For me, anyway.

"I can't believe how much you cuss," Arden says while pounding her keyboard into paste. Some monsters, you take down with skill. Some, you take down with strategy. And some of them? You find out the hard way that you can't kill them at all, so you just keysmash and hope you hit the right buttons to win the day. (This only sometimes works.) (It ain't working right now.)

Jamming on my keys, I say, "No shit I do! You're dying!"

Arden's character drops, and about two seconds later, mine does too. The screen fades to grey, because Warcraft is funny like that. We're both dead and the thing we were trying to kill is back to full life. If we want another go, we'll have to start completely over. But not before we put ourselves back together.

When we reappear on screen, it's ghostly versions of ourselves in a graveyard. We either have to run back and get our bodies or let the graveyard resurrect us. If we let the graveyard angel rez us, though, it breaks all our armor and weakens us so we can't do anything for like, ten minutes.

"What time is it?" Arden asks, then answers herself when she looks at the in-game clock. "Whoa. You wanna just rez tomorrow?"

I've been moving slow for the last couple of pulls. As the healer, it's my job to keep Arden alive while she kills stuff. I have to be alert. And usually, I am. But today ate my lunch and I'm exhausted. What's left of my brain wants to shut down.

I sign out and close the laptop. Then, I lay back on Arden's bed, holding the computer against my chest. It's hot, and the hard drive is still buzzing. Soothing me.

When Arden heaves herself from her chair, she lurches out the door. No idea where she's going, but she disappears down the hall. Her voice hums in the distance; must be talking to Concrete Blocks.

If I'm not gonna ask her to quest with me, I need to get my shit and go. That's a thought I have, but my body doesn't care. I lay there, weighed down with a laptop, letting my eyes close. My thoughts swirl around, tangling and untangling in the quiet. The car's probably still at the gas station. I probably still have a room in Village Estates . . .

Before I can think too much about facing my mother again, Arden comes back. She falls into bed beside me. The motion washes her spicy scent over me. My heart speeds up, excitement and anxiety all together. Are we gonna lay here, all silent again?

"I told Dad you're staying the night," she says. "Basically the one good thing about him being a dick about me. I can have boys in my room *and* shut the door."

The prickly heat of a blush stings my skin. She doesn't mean it like that; there's no way she means it like that. Somehow, I manage to say, "Score one for the silver lining stick."

We lay there a minute; I tell myself I'm ignoring the quiet electricity that hops from my skin to hers. I tell myself she's not feeling it, and I shouldn't be either. I hate being half-right—when she breaks our silence, it's not flirting anymore.

"I don't want to be nosy," Arden says, pushing hair out of her face. "But didn't you have a thing today?"

Weight pulls me down. Invisible, internal. I slide the laptop onto the floor because I don't want to drop it. My throat tight, I try to pick the right words. I guess it's a fair thing to ask.

It's so easy to make up a life on the internet, but I always told the truth about being sick. About dying. Then everything killing me just up and disappearing. All better, clap-clap, jump right back in, Dylan! Probably, Arden was the only one outside my house who knew I was registering on the last day before spring break. So I could go back the same time as everybody else.

Of course she wants to know what happened, because it obviously didn't go like I planned it. Instead, I snuck up on her. Showed up at her door. Reality on the front porch, *knock-knock-knock*. Some part of me wants to roll over and cover her with my body. To stroke her face and tell her if she's even sad a little about all those cancer jokes we used to tell, don't be. But I can't. I'm afraid of her in real life.

So I answer, because she asked. "I went."

"But you didn't stay." She sounds so worried. It's written in her eyes, too. In the slant of her dark brows, marring the pretty roundness of her face.

This should have stayed in the game. Maybe three hours ago, we should have typed this all out. Too late, now. My voice gets thinner as I explain. "I couldn't."

"Why not?"

"Because I'm fucking stupid."

She's restless beside me. Shifting, finally rolling on her side. She tucks an arm under her head and stares at me. Right through me. Her other fingers drum on the mattress. I feel their vibration in the springs—a touch that reaches me, without any physical contact. "Dylan, come on."

"It freaks me out, crowds and shit," I say, and that's one reason. That's the truth.

Arden studies my face. Realizes that's not everything. She sounds hesitant, but she says anyway, "Is that all?"

Nothing hurts, not physically, but all I can think about is the pills I have in my bag. It's like they send up a signal—*hey, you could take us. We could help.*

Those thoughts I shove way down. Instead, I let the rage up—I hate narcotics. I hate them, and I hate all those assholes at school who used to try to buy them off me when I was a freshman. And for that matter, all the douchebags who gave me ten bucks so they could put *their* drugs in *my* locker.

Because nobody's gonna bust me, right? If they do a random locker search, nobody thinks nothing about Cancer Stefansky with a prescription bottle next to his binder. I wanted the money. I *needed* it. So I hated them and took it anyway, and then hated myself some for good measure. A flash of sweat and heat spills over me.

And Arden, because she's good and nice and sweet, asks if I'm okay.

That's what breaks me. Because she looks *at* me when she says it. Her gaze holds mine. Suspended, waiting for an answer, she actually expects one and wants to hear it. I can't remember the last time somebody asked if I was okay and waited to hear the answer. As weird as it is to see her in skin and bones instead of pixels and text, Arden really is the only friend I have left.

"They wouldn't let me register," I admit. Now that the words are out, they rush fast, loose over my tongue. I sit up because I feel like I'm drowning in them. "My mother wasn't there, and they wouldn't let me register."

Arden frowns. "Was she late or something?"

"She worked last night," I tell her. "She figured I could take care of it myself."

This registers on Arden's face. Her soft mouth tightens. There's a hint of her poured-stone father there, hardening her expression. When she talks, her voice is still gentle. Like she's keeping her anger away from me. "Are you serious?"

*As a heart attack*, I want to tell her. A lot of things, I kept to myself. But now, I want to tell her about all the times Medicaid paid for my cab rides home from the clinic because Mom didn't want to drive. And all the times the cab *didn't* show up, because they know if they're coming to a hospice, chances are, they're getting somebody one step from dead or puking in their backseat.

It all bubbles up in my chest, acid and salt, churning and twisting. I grit my teeth. I close my eyes. And I shake my head, because there's some things I don't want to say out loud. Like, if I admit them, it stains Arden somehow. Pushes her farther away. Back into her clean, bright world where shit like that just doesn't happen.

"I don't wanna talk about this," I say.

Settling beside me, I feel Arden shift. Her weight bends the mattress toward her body, pulling me in. She says, "I thought you'd sound different."

I rest my hand on my heart. I like to feel it. Steady, steady, steady. Taking my pulse reminds me that I'm not dying anymore. Not at two in the morning, not at my age. No adverse cardiac events for this boy. My head swirls again; I'm falling asleep. I can't stop it, and I'm not going to try anymore.

I rasp when I finally reply, "Surprise."

# (BEFORE)

**Sometimes when I sleep, my subconscious coughs up** the past. Slices of myself, half-remembered, half-forgotten.

Dozing and dream-addled in Arden's bed, I go back. She's the friend I have now, but when I was little, I had convenience friends. The kids up and down my street, the ones that rode my bus to school.

They came in sibling flocks: four different Carmichaels, a murder of Johnsons. I was the only singleton, so I got to be the tiebreaker. Most of the time, I hung out with Coy Carmichael. She's my age, and she liked to bake stuff. Free cookies if Coy was around.

My mother worked nights then, too. In the summer, she'd come home after her shift, smelling like grease and cigarettes. She'd watch me eat leftover diner pancakes for breakfast. Then she'd send me outside with a cloak of warnings.

*Don't slam the door. Don't make any noise. Don't wake me up unless somebody's bleeding.*

It was all-day freedom, nothing like the kids from High Point that shared our school. They were the ones with new backpacks and bright white shoes. All the time, they had lessons and practices and classes. Their eyes got big and jealous when they found out that we had nothing to do but run the neighborhood. No teachers, no lessons, no rehearsals.

They were the ones who leaned forward when the cop came to school to talk about stranger danger. Like *they* ever had a chance of standing alone on a street corner and being asked to find a lost puppy.

Everybody from Village Estates sat in the back, listening like it was a foreign language. We talked to strangers all day long. People leaning out their car windows, asking for directions. Clerks up at the 7-Eleven, the guys my mom called the Young Turks down at the car wash. Sometimes the owner would give us a couple dollars to dry windshields. Sometimes he threatened to get a gun if we didn't leave. Excitement, bitches. We had it.

Back then, I thought we lived near the woods. Next to a river. After four days of hard rain, the drain that fed it (should have been my first clue that it wasn't a river) gushed out a current strong enough for inspiration.

Coy and I drug a plastic wading pool out of a dumpster to go sailing.

Me and her, we jumped in and it worked. It actually worked. The pool floated with both of us in it, and the current caught us right away. We were *sailing*, bitches. The water tickled through the thin plastic. The pool spun around and around. I remember lights flashing through the reedy trees that lined the culvert. Gold flickers, big as quarters, and we washed by so fast. It was a carnival we could afford. Just ours. All ours. Those kids in High Point could only wish and want.

Screaming and laughing, we thought we might make it to another state. Maybe we would have. But we stopped because somebody called the police. Not on a couple of fourth grad- ers endangering themselves by rafting in the storm drain. But because we were trespassing, and making noise, and far enough from our houses that no one recognized me and Coy. We didn't belong. We were a nuisance.

The same cop who stranger-dangered us at school left his car door open. Walked down the ditch and tossed a piece of concrete block into the water a couple yards in front of us. The pool didn't have brakes, so we washed right into it. The concrete cracked the pool, and water rushed in. The joyride was over.

Clomping down to grab us, the cop bitched under his breath when he got his shoes wet. Yanking my arm up hard to "help" me to shore, he scowled. "Go home," he said. "Don't let me catch you messing around down here again."

His fingerprints on Coy's arm lingered. She was redheaded and speckled, and her skin was thin like tracing paper. She rubbed and rubbed the spot as we walked back up the river. The trip home was slower and steeped in resentment.

"Asshole," Coy whispered. We could run around if we wanted to. Cussing was a different matter. A flyswatter on bare back thighs was no joke, so we kept the mouthiness down low. Backward dog whistle, just loud enough for kids to hear and not adults.

Nodding, I rubbed at my arm too. The marks had already faded, but I wanted them back. It was a badge. Something to show off; we could tell stories about getting arrested. But only if we had proof. Coy's proof flamed on. Mine disappeared under grime and friction burn.

"Double asshole."

Agreeably, Coy said, "His asshole is so big he poops Buicks."

I almost fell down laughing. It hurt my ribs, but I couldn't stop. Officer Friendly who really didn't give a damn about you if you were from Village Estates, not just an asshole but a double-wide. Dissolving into tears on the sidewalk, I grabbed Coy's arm and kept pulling it. Saying it over and over again, I wheezed laughter and hiccupy sobs of delight.

Coy kept trying to top it. Bigger and bigger, meteorites, a whole Venus, Battlestar Galactica—but she'd already won the award. For the rest of forever, when we saw police (and we saw them a lot), they were Buicks.

—*The Buicks are down at Jamie's house again.*

—*Crystal got the Buicks called on her—she was shoplifting Juicy Fruit.*

—*That Buick was looking at your ass.*

That was fourth grade, and in fifth, Coy transferred to Loughner Creek Middle School. Open choice: if your parents felt like doing the forms, they could send you to a different (better) school than the one you got assigned. Me? I went to Virginia

Finch, right down the street. So Coy and I were friends, but not everyday friends anymore. She got a new band of convenience buddies, and I got a diagnosis.

When I first got sick, Coy turned up at my door with a cupcake. She lied and said, "I made too many."

There's no such thing as too many cupcakes. It's just an easy C-word to say, one nobody has to whisper.

That's the last time I saw her, really. At my door, anyway. She still lives down the street. She goes to the better-choice high school, with a better class of people. I watch her leaving with them at night, climbing into their shiny, shiny cars. They laugh, the radio boom-boom-booming as they pass by in slow motion.

Her hair streams out the window and she drives away, further away than we ever sailed together.

# (ALARM CLOCK)

**When I wake up, gravity gives up on me. I fall out of bed;** I hit the ground hard.

The floor is unfamiliar, hard. Pretty, polished wood instead of thin, stained carpet or patterned tile. Nothing smells right; where's the Lysol and the stale air? Where's the off-and-on beeps that go down the hall, echoing at different times?

All this confusion breaks when I hear Arden arguing with her dad. Arden! I'm not at home, and I'm not back at the hospital. I'm a little pin in a map—Amaranth, Pennsylvania—and I blew up what was left of my life yesterday. Shit.

My knees crack as I scramble to my feet. I'm not *trying* to listen to them, but the whole house, all bare wood and glass, amplifies everything. I can even hear my socked feet rasping as I orient myself. The back, panicked part of my brain wants me to gear up and get the hell out. It's always flight with me, never fight.

"They're pants," Arden says, frustrated. There's a wobble in her voice. "They're just pants."

Concrete Blocks wants to know, "What's wrong with jeans?"

I spin in place, searching for my shoes, my *stuff*. I don't know why I can't find them— it's not like my shit is all over the place or anything. Damn it, I want my bag. I just want to have it close. When I spot it, I snatch it up. The bottle inside rattles.

Arden sounds trapped, struggling for a reply. Finally, she coughs up one word, "Nothing."

"Okay great," Concrete Blocks says, like he won the war. "We agree, everybody wears jeans. Why don't you go put some on, then?"

Shit, where can I go, though? Not out the door; they're right outside the door. Like an idiot, I look out the window. It's a long way down, right into rose bushes.

"Whatever," Arden mutters. When she comes in the room, she's not defeated. She's just exhausted. Me, I just stand there, silent.

No big surprise, she doesn't go for the closet; she's not changing the fucking pants. They're nice, they look nice. They're black skinny jeans with big, white flowers printed on them. They go real good with the black-and-white-checked shirt she's layered over them.

I think maybe for a minute she forgot I was even here. She pulls off her headband, her dark curls exploding into a halo around her head. With a swipe across her eyes, she puts herself together and I see the armor go on. I see the deep breath go shallow. Hardness spreads through her shoulders; her spine tightens up. And when she looks up, her green eyes stare right through me.

"Sorry," she says. "I didn't mean to wake you up."

"You didn't."

Everything's tense again, like we didn't spend all last night getting the feel of each other outside the game. I'm holding my bag like it might run from me. She's stretching the shit out of that headband, till the black fabric goes pale and loses its shape. It seems like a long time, but the silence doesn't really last.

Arden melts into motion again. She tosses the headband on her desk. "Yeah, so anyway, welcome to my life."

Everything around us dims. Probably clouds shifting outside the window, it's just weather. But weather changes, and so does a room. Everything that looked clean and rich and perfect to me last night—now it looks like a stop sign. The neat edges warn, *don't touch*. The sharp corners say, *don't get comfortable*. It's not a good place to be sick and sad. It's not a good place.

That realization gives me a flare of courage. I pull the strap of my bag over my neck. "You wanna get out of here?"

"Yeah," she says. She steps into a pair of boat shoes, then looks for her keys. "I noticed you didn't have a car out there. What's up with that?"

The flare feeds a hard, hot seed right in the middle of my chest. It grows, little feelers stretching under my skin. They pulse; they warm. It's that idea, that quest, coming back to life. The one that sounded so good when I was driving, and sounded so stupid when I was elbow to elbow with Arden in the game.

And I dunno, maybe it's the fact that the light shifted. Or maybe it's realizing, even though I could turn around and go home, I don't want to. Or maybe it's some paladin bullshit, thinking I can sweep into this tower and rescue Arden the Good, I don't know. It's a lot of things, and a lot of those things don't even have names or words to go with them. I just feel like maybe Arden never even got a chance to make a wish, let alone turn one down, like I did. This is what we do to feel better: we play the game. We go on quests.

So I say, "You remember the Pearl Ship?" Because we talked about it in the game. We talked about Atlantis, and Avalon, the Bermuda Triangle, and El Dorado—all kinds of places that are supposed to be, or maybe never were.

She squints at me, baffled. "Uh . . . maybe?"

"Yeah you do," I tell her. My hands curve the shape of a galleon in the air. "The one in the desert, the one—"

"Full of pearls," she says. It's obvious she recognizes it now; just as obvious she doesn't know why I'm going on about it. "Sitting out there full of treasure. Waiting for somebody to find it, yeah."

I dart forward. Too fast; she startles. But when I grab her hands, she doesn't pull away. I lower my voice, though, because I don't know where Concrete Blocks is, but I do know how good voices carry around here. "Let's go on a quest, Arden. You're on spring break, right? Let's go find it. You and me, right now. Fuck your dad; let's go. Let's go right now."

She doesn't say *it's just a story*. She doesn't say *you're crazy, we can't, it's impossible, I don't want to, it's a bad idea*, none of that. No. There's no more words; instead, there's motion. Arden sends me to the garage to wait for her. On my way, I liberate all the oranges from the bowl on the kitchen counter.

Fuck me, we're going.

# (DIRECTIONS)

**Leather seats. About a million times, I read books that** talked about buttery leather, and I never got it. What, it's greasy? It's slick? I finally decided on slick. It didn't make sense in context, but what did? Closed up in Arden's car, I get it now. The seats are smooth, almost velvety, and not cold at all. Smooth and creamy and rich and all right, yeah, buttery.

"Nice car," I say when Arden finally slides into the driver's seat. She had to pack and who even knows what she just threw in the trunk. Well, she does. Guess I'll find out. Or maybe not. It's a mystery.

Starting the engine, Arden only sort of nods. "It's my stepmom's old car. She upgraded."

"How do you upgrade a Mercedes?" I ask her. It's a fair question. The peace symbol's right there on the hood, or maybe it's a gun scope. Or propellers. What the hell is it? Now it's gonna bug me until I find out.

"You get a newer Mercedes," she replies.

There's something dark and unhappy in the way she says that. Even though I know why, I can't really wrap my head around it. Every nice thing I have, I hoard like a dragon on top of diamonds. There are days when I'd literally hiss and bite if somebody came for my books or my laptop.

"What did you tell your dad?" I ask.

With a bitter-edged smile, she shrugged. "Said I was going to buy jeans."

We pull out of the garage, and I hear nothing but my breath (labored, no stridor—that means I'm panting, but not whistling and wheezing). It's impossible that a car has an engine this quiet. For once, I shut up.

Clutching the armrest, I squint into pale morning light. It won't settle; it bounces off the hood, off the windows of the houses as we pass by. This car feels like a glass submarine; all the world's blocked out, but all the morning sun flooding in. We skim down the street, and it's not till we get to an intersection that Arden turns to me.

"All right, let's get our quest on. What do I put into the Garmin?" she asks.

"Just get back to I-70."

"But then what?"

"You drive west for, like, a week, then turn left onto I-15."

We're far enough away from the house now that she can smile. It's not even against my will; I smile right back at her. We're blowing this popsicle stand; we're getting the hell out of Dodge. We're alone together now, proper alone, like we are in the game—she scares me; I like it.

"Okay, west for a week, then south for . . . another week? Or what?"

"It's forty some-odd hours if you drive straight through," I tell her. Swimming in my leather seat, I twist beneath the belt. "Or like five days, if we go eight hours a day. We can take I-70 straight to I-15, or we can wander all over, pay a bunch of tolls and drive through endless Dakotas. You know what's in the Dakotas? Nothing. You look up desolate online and you'll get a picture of North Dakota."

"Okay, so you have an I-70 fetish, I get it," Arden teases.

With all the love in my heart, I flip her off. She's so soft and pale; I feel like I can poke a finger right through her skin and stir her up. But I don't. I don't want to. Maybe there are other things I wanna do; that's a thought that pops and sparks, but I leave it alone.

After a light, after a nice little roundabout, Arden leans her head toward me and asks, "How do you know this shit?"

I mean, isn't it obvious? Doesn't she know me? I've spent the last couple years wasting away in bed, with a laptop for my window outside. "A little Googlebird told me."

"Oh, okay, a Googlebird." She reaches out and smacks the back of her hand against my shoulder. Not hard, just like, to change the subject. "You want to stop and get breakfast?"

"We have oranges," I say. Then I add, "I don't have much money."

"Left all your gold in the bank, huh?"

"Yep. But I can pay you back. When I die, you can have my stuff."

If we were in game, that joke would be hilarious. When people get pissy because something's not going their way, they threaten to bail. Like, screw you guys, you can't do this without me. Except, it's a whole game full of people, and yeah we can. So they get wound up, then you make fun of them until they leave. And when they do? You yell after them, "Can I have your stuff?"

It's one of the many ways you can call somebody a pissy little dick in Warcraft without saying it directly. (You have to be sneaky; pissy little dicks report you to the mods.) So then, sometimes you just say it to be funny—just now, I said it to be funny.

But Arden's smile fails. She grips the wheel with both hands, a muscle flickering in her jaw. The pulse fluttering in her throat seems to race; she's stiff all of a sudden. Plastic and molded into place.

That joke in real life? It's not funny. I realize that now, a little too late. Not funny, when I'm sitting next to her, rubbing the knot the PICC line left behind after my last round of chemo.

Not funny after she agrees to go on a quest with me; just not funny. Everything gets heavy. Her eyes fall, like she's reconsidering all of this.

She's crazy if she doesn't. I'm not dying, but I'm not okay. It's really fucking obvious, too. Right now, she's probably worrying—*What do I do? What did I get myself into?* Her expressions are shadows; they flicker across her lips and brow.

Reaching out, I say, "It was a shitty joke, I'm sorry."

Too nice to agree, she makes a soft sound. One that says she heard what I said, but she's not gonna reply.

Now I have to promise. Seal it with a vow. "I won't do it again, all right?"

"All right," she says, her lips flat and pale.

She drives fast, but in the Mercedes, it barely feels like we're moving.

# (DESTINATIONS)

**I don't set out to start a fight. It just happens. *I* keep** sorta happening, and I need to stop.

The greasy haze of hash browns lingers in the air. It competes with the leather, and I have to roll the window down. It's funny—sometimes I can't smell anything, then other times it's all too overpowering. The breakfast that smelled good a half hour ago is turning my stomach now. Touching the button, I look at Arden and say, "Can I?"

"You don't have to ask."

"But can I?" I ask.

"Yes," she says gently. "Of course."

Then, nothing. I get the stink out, roll things back up, and we're silent again.

I'm used to saying things with my hands with her. Crafting my words, being the perfect version of myself in text. Online, I feel like I come across as smart. I say exactly what I mean, clean and smooth. There's no *um*, no *uh*. Everything I type is pronounced right. My grammar's better and there's no hint of a white trash accent.

In person, if I'm tired, or angry or not thinking about it, I can catch myself drawling like hill and holler people, like coal people, because that's my family. Come to a reunion sometime and you'll get your fill of accents—and three different kind of deviled eggs.

Arden's voice is silk.

I dig through my brain to find conversation. I'm bad at this, I realize. I haven't had to do it a lot. Doctors ask questions, and other patients are happy to bitch about the hospital with you. I don't remember the last time I talked to my mother. I don't remember what her voice sounds like when she's not flaring her nostrils and exhaling disappointment.

"There's quest goals on the way. Like, stop at Rock City and commune with seven states of being before you go forth."

With a trace of a smile, she says, "Rock City, huh? Have you been there?"

"I haven't been anywhere. 'Cept the hospital." Warming up now, I tug at my seat belt. It cuts at my neck and I want it off. I have a feeling though, that I'd get a big, sad puppy look if I took it off.

Arden digs her phone out and hands it to me. "Look up the address."

Brushing it aside, I shake my head. "It's in Tennessee. That was just an example. It's not on the way."

"You know that off the top of your head."

"Let me tell you a thing." Settling again, I push the window to let in some air. At first, it feels good. But then the wind rushing in starts to thump. It presses into my eardrums, and vibrates on the seats, and digs into my skin. I know I'm not imagining it because Arden winces, and opens her window a crack.

With everything equaled out, Arden touches my elbow. "Tell me a thing."

"I go on road trips on Google," I say.

"I'm sorry," Arden says. "Explain?"

"The Googlebird. I drive all night on different highways on my computer, so I can give you directions all over. I like the roadside attractions. Like, the headstone capital of the world, or the world's biggest teacup, that kind of shit. I know all of them. I know how to get to them."

She smirks, "Yeah, right."

"You know any? Try me."

She doesn't know any, but I watch her type something into her phone with her thumb. Her gaze darts back and forth from the road as she scrolls. Finally, she looks up in triumph. "The corn palace," she says. Challenge accepted.

"You mean The World's Only Corn Palace? Mitchell, South Dakota. You take I-90 to Highway 37, left on Havens Avenue, right on Sanborn, right *again* on Seventh Avenue, and the parking is free." I don't add, *how about that?* but I kinda want to.

Arden laughs, her eyes lighting up. Once again, she scrolls on her phone, looking for another place to throw at me. She sticks the pink little tip of her tongue out when she does it. It's a perfect triangle, like a kitten nose. I don't love the hell out of it. It doesn't wreck me. It *doesn't*.

"Carhenge."

With a snort, I say, "Alliance, Nebraska, north of I-80. And there's a Foamhenge in Virginia."

Arden hoots with laughter. Her curls bounce, and her smile broadens. Drumming on the steering wheel, she sticks her tongue out again. She hums and murmurs to herself, then lights up. Turning to me, she throws down a challenge. "World's Largest Ball of Twine."

"So easy," I say, pretending to be disappointed. "Darwin, Minnesota—north of I-90, off Highway 12."

Arden taps the brakes; the car shudders. "Wrong!"

Holy shit. Wrapping my arms around myself, I try to squeeze my heart back to a regular beat. It's not a heart attack. It's not even anything. It's just anxiety and surprise, and I don't like being startled. I'm a hypocrite like that. "Uh, not wrong. It lives in a gazebo, in Minnesota, on First Street!"

"It's in *Kansas*," she says, glancing at her phone to be sure. She sounds kinda like she's talking to a slow kid, which I don't appreciate.

"My dick is in Kansas. Lemme see."

"No," she says. She leans away from me, making a face. "I'm right, you're wrong. Just admit it."

"If I was wrong, I would."

"I'm waiting, because you are."

This is why they don't let you drive in kindergarten. I mean, even if you could see over the wheel and reach the pedals. The whole way it would be exactly like this, tiny, hot tempers flaring. Poking each other with metaphorical sticks. My face is red and the blush is spreading to my ears. I can *be* wrong, but she doesn't have to talk to me like I'm an idiot.

I lean against my door. "What'll you give me if I'm right?"

"A ride to California," she says.

That's when I start to doubt. Is this a dream? A hallucination? Is this everything that's happening in the last blink of my eye?

Maybe I didn't get better. Maybe this is the last coma. Anxiety winds a chain around my neck; it pulls it tight. I don't want this to be made up. I need this. I need her and suddenly I hate her for making me doubt all of it.

Thrusting out my hand, I say, "I have to call my mom."

That tears a hole right through the moment. Arden's expression fades to neutral. Curls waver around her face, a dark halo as the wind streams through the windows. I don't even want the air anymore; it smells like oil and worn-out road.

Reading my mind, Arden closes the windows and the car seals tight as a mason jar once more. Then she hands me the phone.

Dialing with just my thumb, I listen to the ring. Only twice, and then *she* picks up, my mother. Her voice crackles, not because the connection is bad. That's just how she sounds, like ice cubes settling in a glass of warm water.

"Who is this? Is that you, Dylan?" she demands. Her voice cuts, the brittle edge of something sharp. Holy shit, she's pissed.

My palms sweat; I shrink in my seat, growing smaller and smaller. If I compress myself enough, maybe I'll disappear. Panic zings around my skull, electric and terrifying. My mouth won't open and I don't say anything, which worries Arden. I know this, because she reaches toward me. Plaintive and strained, she prompts, "Say something."

It's just loud enough that my mother hears it. Her tone changes, now wary instead of impatient. "Bobby?"

Before I can say no, or correct her, or try to explain or anything, she explodes. Her anger fills the car, bitter and bright. "God-damn it, I know that's you, Bobby! I want my two hundred dollars, you hear me?"

Hearing that is a punch to the throat. Bobby is her boyfriend, except when he's not. He's been in and out the last couple of years.

Allegedly, he's a musician. Point in his favor: he has a guitar. Point against his favor: there's a handwritten sign in his truck window. It says he'll haul away anything for fifty dollars, no questions asked. I'm pretty sure Bobby's real job is scrounging. And, apparently, borrowing.

But here's what I wanna know: where, exactly, did my mother get two hundred dollars to lend to a dillweed like Bobby?

That question sharpens my teeth and hardens my flesh. On the outside, I feel contorted, like I walked out of a funhouse mirror. On the inside, it's nothing but hatred and flames and gall, because last week, all my toast was stale bread from the outlet store. *We didn't have the money for groceries,* she said.

"I can hear you breathing, you son of a—"

I hang up. The phone's case is heavy in my hand. All over, I'm hot and tensed, like I've been running. I'm even out of breath. Flush with humiliation, I can't stand to look over at Arden. An idiot, I dragged my stupid, ugly life right into her lap. I'm afraid if I look at her, I'll see disgust.

"*She* sounds nice," Arden says, deadpan.

It breaks me out of my shock; I even laugh a little. "Oh yeah. The best."

Finally breathing right again, I shake the phone like it might cast the demons out. Then, I look up twine to settle the question once and for all. It turns out my mother's a liar, and I'm a know-it-all asshole who can't even get it right.

Reading out loud from Wikipedia, I tell Arden, "There are several claims to the world's biggest ball of twine."

"Oh," she says.

"And you know what sucks?"

"What?"

Turning the ringer off, I drop the phone in the console. Any-time now, my mother's gonna call back. She's drawing off the air in this car. She's going all the way to California with me, croaking on my shoulder, and it's all my fault.

Exhausted with my own stupidity, I roll my head and tell Arden, "Ain't neither one of 'em on I-70."

I'm white trash, and sometimes I sound like it.

# (TOASTERS, PICKLE PLATES)

**Some force drags me forward, and the seat belt locks.**
It's not until I wake up that I realize I was asleep. In time, my
head throbs and my heart pounds. What happened? I was just
*gone*, like that. What if I never came back? What a waste of last
words, what a waste of everything—

"Take a picture," Arden says, handing me her phone.

I clear my head with a shake and look around. There's nothing
worth shooting that I see. Then, Arden's hand moves into my
space. She pushes my wrists in the right direction. A hulking
cement wall fills the horizon. It looks like the back side of a
prison, or a scene from a Russian mob movie or something.

That's when I see the looping cursive sign on top. From my vantage, it's backward. Still legible, though. I shift the phone to make sure I get the words in there. Breezewood Motel. I wait for the right angle, my finger hovering over the button.

"Take the picture or I'll want to stay there," Arden says. "I love ugly, cheap motels."

"Yeah, well you got both with that one, all right." When I touch the screen, there's a click. Then I lean into her side of the car to show her the picture. "I think we ought to anyway. If we wait until morning, we can rob all the vampires that live there."

Arden's laughter is low and warm. It teases my ear. "I think that's where the Occupy vampires crash. They're the ninth century *and* the ninety-nine percent."

"Yeah," I say, turning the AC vent right on me. "Yeah, why's everybody think vampires are rich anyway?"

Arden considers this. "They never have to buy groceries."

"Three hundred years of rent," I counter.

"Maybe they sell their stuff. To museums."

"Oh yeah. Everything they own is antiques."

"My *stepmom* takes trips," she says suddenly. Expressions flicker across her face, too many to count, too fast to register. "Like weekend trips, just to buy antiques."

I didn't meet Stepmom. Thinking back hard, I try to remember what Arden told me about her family. For some reason, she lives with her dad instead of her mom, which makes no sense considering Concrete Blocks can't even deal. Seems to me like Arden said her mom was living in another state, maybe. Too far to visit, anyhow. That, I know. As for the stepmom, I don't remember word one about her. And that's . . . strange.

Beside me, Arden's still fired up. If a current passed through her, she couldn't twitch more. It's something to watch and I want to know what kind of antiques could make her this crazy.

So I ask—how do you find anything out, unless you ask? "Like what kind?"

"Depression glass, mostly." She flicks on her turn signal.

There's nobody around us—it's the hazy side of late afternoon, and there are cars, yeah. But we could weave back and forth between the lanes if we wanted to. I wonder if that's something

Arden ever wanted to try. Considering how much she likes riding the brakes, probably not. But maybe. Maybe later, I'll ask her.

"What, sad bottles? Misery plates?" I go ahead and ask. "What the hell is depression glass?"

When Arden laughs this time, it's vaguely annoyed. Not at me. It's thin and bitter, rolling through her words when she finally speaks. "Dishes. Cheap dishes they made during the Depression. According to Mona, they gave away this stuff in boxes of oatmeal, or if you bought a tank of gas, here, here's a free plate. Stuff like that. Like a toaster when you get a checking account."

"Do they really do that?" I ask. I don't have a checking account. Or savings. Or anything. Because I don't have any money. My mother doesn't either—or wait, I guess she does since there was that two hundred dollars to throw around, but whatever. There's nothing in the account (*allegedly*) and they stopped taking our checks at the Red Stripe long before they stopped taking checks altogether (*factually*).

From the sound of her voice, Arden doesn't realize I was asking about the toaster for real. She just goes on, her voice rising. "She rents a car, or flies out to New York or whatever, to pay a thousand bucks for a pickle dish that somebody's great-grandmother got at Woolworth's for free."

A thousand might as well be a million; she's talking about crazy numbers. Before I can ask her if she's serious, or why we're getting off the highway, she explodes.

"It's a plate with handles on it that you put pickles on! And it's not for anything! It sits in a cabinet all day, because you can't eat from it, obviously! It's worth too much!"

Without thinking, I reach over to rub her knee. Just to try to comfort her or something. The curve off the highway is sharp and she needs both hands on the wheel. I ask, softly, "So, we hate her, huh?"

Color tinges the curve of Arden's ears. I see it, peeking through the dark waves of her hair. It spreads down, staining her cheeks, and then she sighs. "No. She's fine. I spend the money my dad gives me, too."

We coast to a turn, and then we're on this highway that goes right through—I'm guessing—Breezewood. Everything looks sad and dingy, too much like my neighborhood, to be honest. The vampire motel was the highlight. When the quiet stretches out too long, I turn the AC up some more. "Where are we going?"

"We have to do this jog before we can get back on 70, that's all. We'll be in Ohio in a couple of hours."

"We had a plan, boo! What were you doing when I was asleep?" I demand, but kidding. There was never any reason to get off 70, but she's wound up enough that I just want her to be happy again. And if she has to pay a couple tolls, well, that's her fault, isn't it?

For a second, I think Arden might break down. Then this serene calm comes over her. It's almost like a glow; she shines from the inside. She shrugs, "Wouldn't you like to know?"

"Always," I reply. I sound like a cheap trick.

Nodding ahead, Arden points out, "Close to Ohio, now."

It's almost embarrassing how excited I am to see that sign. In my lifetime I've been to DC and Pennslyvania—probably West Virginia, too, but I don't remember it.

Ohio, though? Not ever. A new state. A new world.

"Hey," I say, getting brave. I brush my hand against her arm, on purpose. I like it when she touches me; I like touching her back. God help me.

She replies, "Hey."

"Thanks for this."

Everything dark burns away when she smiles.

# (ROAD CONVERSATIONS)

**"So, this boat we're looking for," Arden says.**

Her hands must be tired, because now she's steering with her knees. It's kinda cracked out how comfortable she is, driving when she's doing sixty things besides driving. If she'd quit hitting the brakes at random, I'd probably be that relaxed, too.

Me, I'm touching all the shiny things on the dashboard. "It's not a boat; it's a galleon."

With a smirk, Arden says, "I'm Muggle-born, what do I know about galleons?"

"Ha ha ha," I reply, making a face at her. "What about the ship, Arden?"

"You mean the—" she cuts herself off, fighting back laughter. "Okay, seriously though, okay. The captain steals the pearls, he gets lost up the river, now they're in the desert. All that part, I get. How do we *know*?"

"What do you mean, how do we know?"

"If he sailed out there and got stuck, then how do we even know the story? Wouldn't it just be some ship that got lost at sea? I mean, we wouldn't even know about the pearls; there wouldn't have been anybody left to tell that part of the story."

"They didn't die because they got stuck," I insist. "They walked out of the desert . . ."

"Because they were prepared for that. Sounds fake, but okay."

"They just were," I insist. "They walked out, and they had to go back to Spain and get the money to try to come back and recover it. It takes a whole year, but when they get back, the sand swallowed it."

"All right, so at this point, have they realized California is not an island? Or did they sail another ship up the same river that got them stranded in the first place?"

She's laughing, and I'm laughing—it's just the way she's asking the questions. You have to be here, I guess.

I press a hand to my chest, "It's not my story. I'm just telling you what happened. He sailed on in, took a wrong turn at Albuquerque . . ."

"That's in New Mexico," Arden says sagely.

"Jesus, it's an expression!" Now I laugh, my smile fixed as I boggle at her. In the game, she talks plenty. But because we have all our conversations in text, she can't interrupt. Sometimes we wander off topic (*weird things that scare you, go: Arden says blue jays, I say helium balloons*), but the back-and-forth goes, well, back and forth. This is interesting . . . it's different.

Finally putting her hands back on the wheel, Arden takes a deep breath and then slumps when she lets it out. "Okay, go on."

Then—as fast as I can—I retell the story and put in as much logic as I can. How the river was too shallow, how Iturbe abandoned his riches thinking he could come back to it, how wrong he was, all of it. By the time I spit it all out, I'm lightheaded. I've never talked this fast in my life. My ears are seriously ringing, and my throat's a little sore. But I'm pretty fucking puffed-up because that was a world-record monologue, and Arden was there to hear it.

"That sounds like an urban legend."

"Did it end with a hook in your car door?" I demand. "Or the call coming from inside the house?"

Shrugging, Arden grins. "I never really got that one. I call my dad from inside the house all the time."

"Listen," I say, officially distracted. "The people in the story have a landline. So if the call came from inside the house . . ."

"Then the killer has a cell phone, and the operator wouldn't know that."

Huh. I roll that over in my head a minute, and come to the conclusion that the pretty girl who doesn't let a guy finish his stories is, in fact, right. "Yeah, I guess so."

Pleased, Arden leans her head toward me. "This ship of legends, then . . ."

"It's real. People have seen it."

"Friend of a friend?" she teases.

"It's real," I tell her, and I grin when she hits the brakes yet again.

# (2484.69)

**Hills and high banks of trees darken an already dark** road. It feels like sliding out of a coat when we cross the state line—too hot before, but too cold now. I'm tired, nothing new. Arden's flagging, though. We done crossed state lines, on a road trip she didn't realize she was taking.

"You wanna stop?" I ask.

Changing lanes, mostly for the variety I think, Arden shakes her head. It slowly turns to a nod, and she looks to me. "Important question time. Boring-but-decent or no-tell motel?"

Sometimes it's hard to carry on a conversation, the two of us, but questions like that prove we are who we are. Who we always have been together. Before, our quests took us up mountains speckled with fire elementals. Now it's along a dark path in Ohio, speckled with McDonalds (McDonaldses?) We quest on, pillagers of the Pearl Ship, in search of an inn for the night.

"You like the weird motels," I say. It's a new fact about her, shiny and bright. I roll it on my tongue, and it tastes so sweet when she smiles in recognition. I kinda wanna hold her hand, but she doesn't act like she wants me to, and it's different, in skin. In the game, when we flirt with each other, come on to each other with emotes and gestures, it can't lead anywhere. It's safe, I guess.

My body, next to her body—it's confusing. I don't remember a time when I wasn't into guys; even in preschool when you just love everybody and have special friends, I wanted to sit next to boys. And that's not Arden, no matter what she got assigned at birth. Wanting to hold her hand makes me feel like I'm lying—to her? To me?

But it goes around again; we're inseparable in the game, but this isn't the game, but you kinda have to love somebody you spend every night with, but did we really spend that together, when we were made out of nothing but electricity and light?

It's not solvable; I keep my hand to myself.

We pass a couple of chains, lit up bright and parking lots full. Every time, Arden shakes her head and laments—too much tell in that motel.

You should see the way she lights up when we find the Baytes Motel—I'm not kidding. That's really the name. It's a cousin to the cinderblock sadness that was the Breezewood—a narrow brick building, single-story, punctuated by a door, a window. Space, then a door, and a window. On and on, all the way down the gravel lot.

Somebody tried to plant flowers around the motel's sign, but the blooms are exhausted. Daffodils lay on the thin grass, too tired to stand.

"I got this," Arden says, barely parked before she's rolling out of the car. I try to follow her shape in the dark. At the right angle, I see her standing at the front desk. She rubs the back of her neck with one hand, talking and talking to a clerk I can't see.

When she comes back, she drives us three doors down and hands me the key. Hanging from a thick plastic disk, the key is grungy. Even the key, yes. The lock it fits into feels . . . insubstantial. If I wanted to, *I* could bust through this door. What's to stop malcontents and bad guys from doing the same?

We're waving a big red flag, parking a Mercedes right outside #4.

It's not like the bad guys even need that much incentive. My mother got a refurbished flat screen from one of her friends, put the box out at the corner with the rest of the trash. Next day, broken window in the back of the apartment and no TV.

Lynne stood in our dining room, an ash trailing off her cigarette as she sighed. "People just can't have nice things anymore."

"It's probably those High Point honor students," my mother replied. That's what she always says so she doesn't get caught saying something racist, which is what she means.

We didn't call the police, because they wouldn't come. Or if they came, they would just write some stuff down and then disappear. No fingerprint dust in Village Estates. None of that eerie blue glow spray they use with the black lights. If a tree falls in a forest and there's no one to hear, does it make a sound? If a television goes missing on the shit side of town, does anybody care?

This is why I sleep with my laptop between my mattress and box spring. And I don't even know why I'm thinking about this, except, I guess, the Baytes Motel reminds me of home in the worst way.

Our room seems like a good place to die in a vintage porn movie. One wall is wood-grain panels, the other three? Yeah, baby, concrete block. Painted a faint shade of yellow, or maybe they were white once. It's hard to say. The TV here is bolted to the dresser, and maybe that's something we should have tried back home.

The remote is bolted to the side table, along with the lamp. It never would have occurred to me that a lamp might be worth stealing. But who knows? We had a couple kids last year breaking into empty units and stealing the plumbing. Zinc and copper is worth something at the scrap yards, and Lynne said it was the landlord's fault that they hadn't updated to plastic pipes like the rest of the world.

"This is . . . ," Arden says.

She doesn't finish. Is it because a room like this is more than her brain can process? All that talk about loving the low rent, it could have just been talk.

The quiet goes on too long, so I offer up a word. "Terrifying?"

All at once, Arden breaks into a smile. "Awesome!"

Whatever froze her in place has set her free, and now she's

flitting all over the room. She drops on the bed, and I'm almost disappointed for her that it doesn't squeak. She doesn't stay there, though. In a second, she's back on her feet. She pokes into drawers, opens the closet. When she darts into the bathroom, she reappears almost immediately. "There's a bottle opener on the wall in here."

I can't help it; she's slumming it and loving it, and it makes me laugh. As I settle in on the bed, I ask her, mock serious, "Are you judging people who need to drink on the can?"

She lets her backpack slip from her arm. Sitting down beside me, she takes in all the glory. The bedspread, rust red with big green flowers on it, is shiny from cheap polyester and fireproofing. Low, bumpy carpet shows off a variety of stains that, I'm not gonna lie—somebody did try to clean them up. They're outlines of spills now, little Coke crime scenes unintentionally remembered. One long look from cinder block to cinder block, then Arden beams. "I can't believe this place is only forty-nine dollars a night."

Forty-nine?? That's a lot. Almost all the cash I have in my pocket; all the money I have in the world. When we stopped for gas, I didn't offer to pay for any, and I didn't even try to pony up for the room. Am I a terrible person, taking advantage?

As happy as she is, I feel guilty. "Maybe tomorrow we should sleep in the car to make up for it."

There's something funny in the way Arden doesn't reply immediately. She studies my face. I can see some kind of decision happening. Her dark eyes soften and she lays back, tucking her hands under her hair. "We can. If you want to."

She's warm next to me; she smells nice. Clean in a way this room never has been. If she can leave a trace behind, it'll be a better memory than the other people left. *Arden Trochessett was here.* Left it better than she found it. Sweeter than the metallic breath that the window-unit AC pumps out. All at once, I don't care how confusing she is. I wanna kiss her. There's no way I'm gonna kiss her.

Instead, I ask, "How do you say your last name?"

Like a smart-ass, she replies, "Your last name."

I want to tattoo her into my skin, *things I can't,* a reminder. And to make sure I don't try something she probably doesn't want me to try, I press one finger between her ribs to make her squirm. It's not a tickle; it's an irritation. A poke. Enough to make her sit up and slide farther across the bed. When she flops down again, she does it on one side. With one arm and a pillow, she protects the other. Safe from me; away from me, she answers my question. "Tro-sheh-say. Like, say hey."

"Hey, Trochessett."

"Hey to you, too," she answers, and melts onto her back.

# (CONNECTED)

**I'm broken into angles. My head rubs against Arden's**
shoulder, but my torso points away. Hips, they're turned toward
her again; I'm a triangle, laying near her, not on her. Music
thrums through the thin walls, vibrations that feel like bees on
my skin. I keep drifting back and forth—awake, not awake.

"All his teeth sharpened to points," Arden says, waving a hand
as she talks. She shifts, and her weight shakes the bed as she
turns to look at me. "And get this. His hair is . . . it's not white.
It's clear, I swear to god, it's like silky fishing line . . ."

The weird, drifting place of sleep-not-sleep lets the conversation
stray. I'm not sure what we're talking about. All I have on offer
is trivia. "Polar bears have clear fur."

"Seriously?"

"And black skin. There are black-skinned chickens, too. But how would you know?"

"You're blowing my mind here, Sutty. I mean, Dylan."

Oh, that's right. Until last night, I wasn't real to her, either. This Dylan person, taking up space in a bed she paid for, he's imaginary. But getting realer, I guess—I smile when she calls me my real name; I roll toward her. When I do, I catch a hint of her scent—spicy and good. I never met anybody who smells as good as Arden does; it actually makes my heart buzz. "Either or, it's all me."

Everything is still. In the quiet, I can almost make out the song playing next door. Only almost—it's familiar but I can't place it. Arden's breath is warm on my hair; it's a touch that's not a touch—she probably doesn't even realize she's doing it. But I do, and I wish it was her hand, or her lips. Sleep sinks down again, pulled away when Arden tugs on the collar of my hoodie. Her knuckles graze my throat.

"You didn't eat any pizza," she says.

"I'm still full from lunch."

It's not really true. I don't do *hungry* the way I used to. I do get an ache, a groan in my belly—my body keeps track of what I *need*. Unfortunately, my brain is in charge of what I *want*, and right now, I want impossible things.

Arden is sweet, and she believes my lie. Lunch was another state ago, a shared sandwich at a roadside stand. We stopped for the novelty, and because Arden felt like daring salmonella. Looks like she won though, she's fine. Pink and flush and suddenly moving. Pushing off the bed, she dumps the pizza box in our fridge. Then she sweeps back. The bedsprings protest faintly when she falls in beside me.

When she does, she curls toward me, and I put a hand between us. Against her chest, and it's already done when I realize that maybe I shouldn't have. Her heart is right there, underneath my hand, and I just did it, like I had a right to. There's her pulse, smooth and regular. I feel it thrumming beneath her shirt. I feel each breath she takes, exhales. I stare at her collarbone, because I'm afraid to look into her eyes. She'll read my mind.

"What are you thinking?" she asks me.

Never. Never am I gonna tell her I'm thinking about her skin and her mouth and how I know I'm not allowed to want her. So instead, I say something that will push us far, far away from dangerous things. "You were checking your phone before; heard from your dad?"

"Yeah," Arden says. It's like she's trying to be light about it, but bitterness creeps in anyway. "Wanted to know how long it takes to buy a pair of jeans."

"Did you tell him about a hundred twenty hours, give or take?"

She snorts. "No. I told him we met up with some friends. I'm good for another night."

"Nice."

Arden curls toward me. Her knees brush mine and she sort of covers my hand with hers. *Warm.* She burns like a furnace. It makes me sweat, being so close, but it's a natural heat. It's good. "There's a bunch of texts . . ."

"Delete 'em." Now I do raise my eyes; I roll a shoulder. "It's my mother; I don't wanna talk to her."

"No, really?" Arden says, a slip of a smile touching her lips.

"I'm a pain in the ass like that," I tell her. "A menace."

"Oh yeah? Well, lucky me: I love a menace."

We're the same, the two of us. All this time, all this empty space in us, we've been filling it up together. Hours and hours in the game, with magic and meandering walks to our next quest, talks late into the night about whatever stupid thing came to mind. This is just evidence of it, whispered as the AC roars to life again.

I let the very tips of my fingers press lightly against her soft skin. That's as much as I dare. And we lie there together in the dark. We listen to other people's music and car tires on gravel, coming and going. Going and coming.

All hours of the night, until it lulls us both to sleep.

# (SECTION 8 PHYSICS)

**It's my fault. I'll say that up front.**

Morning rolls in like fog, hazy except for a bright spot of plea-sure. I don't need an alarm clock today. Arden's plastered to my back, one heavy arm slung across my waist. Her fingers graze against my belly; sometime in the night, my shirt got rucked up to bare my skin. Her breath says stay; it falls evenly on my wiry hair. When she inhales, her body tightens against mine. Now I'm awake, and my body's tight a whole new way.

Strangers touch me all the time. They grab my arms and roll their thumbs across my veins. On my face, thumping my back . . . they help me into wheelchairs and out of beds. Onto blue pleather bench-chairs with extendo-arms, lashing me down so they can push needles under my skin. There's so much touching, but it's all brief. Indifferent. I could be meat or a box of groceries or a bag of bones. Nobody lingers.

Though Arden's sleeping, this feels deliberate. Her arm around me on purpose, connected.

Sometimes, you want things and know you're never gonna get them. Sometimes, rarer, you get something you didn't expect. I want to bury myself in Arden's arms and fall asleep again.

But my bladder has other ideas. Reluctantly, I slide off the bed. When my feet hit the floor, they burn. Walking through embers, I curse quietly. Sometimes, I only *imagine* I'm hurting. Side effect from the chemo. While it was destroying everything in its path, it didn't stop to go *oh hey, he might need these nerve endings later.*

Nope. Zap! Moving on!

You would think, no more nerve endings, no more pain, right? Sorry, no. Because there's no signal and my brain thinks there should be one, *so it makes one up.* And let me tell you, it never makes up *awww, the soft feeling of a puppy pile.* It's more along the lines of *carpet covered in pushpins and thumbtacks.*

After the bathroom, I come back into the room and I'm disappointed. In my absence, she shifted. Now she's sprawled facedown, clinging to a pillow. That moment, that perfect moment waking up in her arms, that's gone now.

So that sucks, and my stomach decides to give a twist. I scoop the change off the dresser and head out to the vending machine. Sometimes a nice, icy Coca-Cola makes everything better. Maybe it'll taste like something today! Breakfast of kings and queens and soon, me. Cold pizza to go with; it's almost like I made it to college or something.

With a hand pressed against the jamb, I open the door. I figure I can squeeze out, grab my soda, and get back into bed before Arden wakes up. It's a plot, vaguely nefarious. As my eyes adjust to the angle of the sun, I wonder if I'm taking advantage of her. No, I don't have to wonder. I am. I know that.

It's wrong to ask for more. It's wrong to want a part of her heart while I'm at it. Nothing stops me from wanting it, though.

Sometime last night, she moved the car. The space in front of our room is empty, a crumpled pack of Camel Menthols decorating it. I shuffle to the vending machine and spend all of Arden's change, but I do get two cans. Two. *See?* I tell myself. *You can think of other people, and sometimes you even do.*

It's not till I get back to our door that I realize—wait, the parking lot is empty. There's a semi parked at the far edge of the gravel, still idling. It hums low, competing with chattery morning birds. The white Chevy that sat in front of the office last night sits there, still. Dew hazes the windows, thick enough that I could sign my name in it.

"Why'd you move the car, Arden?" I ask her, though I'm talking to myself.

Turning, then turning again, something flashes in the gravel. Bright. Brilliant. Maybe it's a diamond, I think idly. You never know when you might find something good on the ground. I found a ten dollar bill on the playground once. Crumpled into a green nugget, it fit perfectly inside my fist.

The glint in the lot though, is not jewels. It's glass. Greenish, perfectly square chunks. Not very much of it; I swallow hard. When you bash a car window in, most of the glass goes inside the car. Steal the car, the glass goes away with it. Physics, Village Estates style.

It's just a fact in my neighborhood— don't leave anything good in your car. And don't bother locking the doors, because sometimes kids only want a joyride. They drive it out of gas, and leave it on the side of the road. A lot of times, you get it back.

And if you locked it, you'll have to replace the window when you do.

Anxiety grips me. Arden's Mercedes isn't the same as my mother's fifteen-year-old Monte Carlo. It's a rich car. A fancy car. It *matters* if it's gone!

Oh fuck, it's gone, our ride is gone. That nice car, all leather and air conditioning that works and stereo so good the bass thumped all through my body—it's stolen. In the middle of the night, maybe a hundred feet from our bed. How did we sleep through it? Why didn't she have an alarm? Or maybe she did; it's not hard to cut the wires on one. (You hear stuff where I live.)

Tears spring up, angry and hot. It's not fair, but so what? Life isn't fair. We're trapped in the middle of nowhere at the Baytes freaking Motel. In Ohio. What was I thinking, when I thought we could make it to California? What the hell? I was out of my mind!

"No, no, no," I say it over and over, like my voice is out of my control. My face is hot and slick, and that awful, warbling sound falls from my lips. Arden's voice comes soft and right behind me.

"Oh my god."

"I'm sorry," I say. I push a soda into her hands and duck back into the room. I'm hiding in the awful, wet-aluminum, cinder-block, wood-paneled jail cell that's the end of the line.

The quest. This friendship. This . . . something more.

I killed it. All of it.

Arden will never forgive me.

I don't know if I can forgive myself.

# (iT'S IMPORTANT TO SECURE YOUR PASSWORD)

**She follows me. She has to; it's not like she can drive** away.

"I can't believe they stole the car."

Oh, I can. She's flapping around like a bird with a broken wing, and it's clear nothing like this has ever happened to her before. I scrub my face with a hand towel from the bathroom. It smells like harsh soap and cigarette smoke. It's rough, and it rasps on my skin. Cleaning everything off, leaving me red and raw, it's like punishment and correction all in one.

"I'm sorry," I tell her again. "I shoulda warned you about a place like this. I shoulda said something. I'm sorry."

My thoughts nag—*You should have left her in Amaranth. You should have left her alone. You're dragging her down, boy, all the way down into the dark. Look at you, shame on you, you're as bad as Mom.*

"Stop apologizing," she says, sort of snappy. "We have to think."

Her irritation cauterizes me. It's unexpected; I didn't realize she had barbs at all. I mean, inside the game, she's hardcore and hilarious; she makes dead baby jokes. She's made dead *me* jokes. But that was in fun. This is real.

*Real was what you wanted, wasn't it?*

I drop the towel on the bed and pull my shit together. She's got her phone out now, and that makes sense. The cops probably care if somebody steals a Mercedes, but I know a couple things from experience. "Okay, um. Call the station, not 911, that's for people dying and shit. They'll come out and take a report."

Her eyes turn sharp. Arden squints, baffled. Baffled *at* me, like I just turned stupid or blue. "I'm not calling the police."

Well, that's it. The stress of real life done broke her brains. Twenty-four hours on the road, and she's already lost it. Sympathy wells in me; I'll talk her down. She needs it, obviously. Reaching out for her, I say, "They're not bringing it back, Arden."

"I didn't think they would," she informs me. "But I can log into it on my phone. It's got a tracker; they can turn it off by satellite."

My mouth drops open. I hear the words coming out of her mouth. I even recognize them. But that's the craziest, science-fiction-est shit I've ever heard in my life. There she is, screwing around on her phone like she's on the deck of a starship and I'm drooling like the yokel that aliens abducted from the cow yard.

"Shit," she says.

Brows lifting, I lean forward. At this point, I kinda can't wait to find out what she says next. Maybe jet fighters are gonna scramble and bring the Mercedes back. Why not? It would make about as much sense. "What?"

Incredulous, she waves the phone at me. "They hacked it. I can't log in."

"They hacked your car."

Groaning, Arden drags a hand down her face. "They hacked the car. Damn it, damn it, damn it."

My hand falls on her arm. I was going for her shoulder, but this works. Squeezing it gently, I catch her eye. I can be reasonable,

I tell myself. I can be helpful and thoughtful and all that, I can. As gentle as I can, I go on. "Then you're gonna have to call the police. Insurance won't pay for it if you don't file a report."

Arden claps her hand over mine. Instead of brushing it away, she holds it there. Now she's the one in charge, the one who's calm. She doesn't search my face; she looks right in my eyes. Steady and sweet, she explains, "If I report it, we'll never make it to California."

"I . . . what?"

Hope is a salt knot, caught in my throat. Of course you tell the cops that somebody stole your robot car. Of course she goes home, where shit like this never happens. This quest is over, isn't it? Is it not?

"The cops will go straight to my dad; the car's registered in his name. Dylan, he doesn't give a shit if I leave for a while, but he'll lose it over the car." She pauses. "I'm not ready to go home. Are you?"

"You're sure." I don't ask; it's flat disbelief. I thought maybe she'd make it maybe as far as Indiana or even Missouri before she took off. Fled for the comfort of Mercedes-land and Apple-land and rooms-that-probably-weren't-the-scene-of-a-murder-in-the-seventies-land. But she's staying? She wants to keep going? For the second time in as many days I find myself wondering if I'm dreaming this.

With a squeeze, Arden lets go of my hand and turns a tight circle. It's like she's summoning something, thinking with her body, something. When she stops, she swipes the screen of her phone, then jabs at it. Suddenly, the room is full of dial tone.

"What are you doing?"

She stares at me, all business. "Creating an alibi."

The speaker *clicks*. "David?" a man says. "You're up before noon."

"Yes, sir," Arden replies stiffly. Her posture shifts ever so slightly. "Dylan's mom got breakfast, doughnuts, you know."

Pinning my lips closed, I listen in disbelief. Yesterday, Arden said we were hanging out, so she wasn't coming home, and that was no problemo. Wow. He gives about as much a shit as my mom does. They should hang out.

When Arden's talking to her father, her spine rolls out to its full height. With her shoulders back, her clothes tighten against her skin. Her rumpled tunic clings, and she becomes somebody else—an empty, military version of herself. Her spark, her crazy, beautiful spark, is completely gone. "Yeah, so anyway, I wanted to check in before we headed out to the lake house."

Arden's dad *hmms*, something clicking away behind him. A keyboard, maybe? It sounds like he's messing with stuff on a desk, barely listening. "Refresh my memory."

Pointing at the phone, Arden says, "I told you about it at dinner. Last week, when Mona was in Atlantic City."

"Right, right, of course. It's been a busy season; I should have put it on the calendar."

It's a Jedi mind trick in real life, unfolding right in front of me. Slowly sitting on the edge of the bed, I stare. In awe, for real. Even *I* couldn't get away with something like that. My mother couldn't care less about what I do, but she remembers every single detail of every single thing ever. Mainly so she can throw whatever's got the most spikes back in my face.

Once, I threw up beside her car—not *in* it, next to it. All the way home, she wouldn't shut up about how, when I was little, everybody thought I was allergic to strawberries for the longest time because I puked every time I ate them, and that one time I puked right in the backseat of the car, and it smelled for months after, and that strawberry puke is red and terrifying, and she paid out the ass to take me to the hospital over it. *Twice.*

She remembers every time I kept her up at night, and every time I didn't, and every little thing I did that made her life hard and how it was my fault Charlie—my dad— walked out on her . . . If I could give my mother amnesia like this, she'd be catatonic. Staring at the walls in silence, digging at the knees of her polyester work pants like she was haunted.

"Probably the whole week," Arden says. Her voice is restrained, but she moves restlessly. She take sharp steps as she stalks through the room. Her reflection wavers; the mirror is imperfect. "You only get one spring break, right?"

Arden's father hums again. His voice trails away, distracted. "Put it all on the Amex. Mona's saving points to go to Cabo."

"Yes sir," Arden says. Silence floats, drifting in the place where somebody should say good-bye. Instead, there's a click, and the line goes dead.

"He . . . he bought that," I say, still amazed.

"Always does." With a flourish, Arden bows to me. She's a

marionette, her motions precise but unnatural. "Ta-da!"

Impulsively, I catch her face between my hands. My touch strays; her hair is softer than it looks. It slips between my fingers, twining, tangling. I can't take my eyes from her lips, the ones that lied so smoothly, so convincingly. It would be so simple to just lean in and—

She laughs, and it breaks the spell. I raise up on my toes and kiss the tippy-top of her head. In response, she shoves me gently. I tumble back onto the bed, knocked over, knocked out and smiling. I cross my hands over my sternum, a vampire. It's wrong to be happy right now. Arden's father sucks. She just proved that. And her car is who knows where?

But it doesn't matter. I *am* happy, because this quest goes on. It's not over—she doesn't *want* it to be over, not just yet anyway. Not when we're still only in Ohio. Pointing a toe, I stretch my leg out and swing it until I bump into her. Bump, bump, I don't even lift my head. "I'm gonna make this up to you."

"Yeah, yeah. I don't know what we're going to do now, though," she admits. She catches my ankle and holds my foot aloft. "I can't buy a car with a credit card."

She probably *could* buy a car with that thing. But chances are her father would get a call about that. Luckily, I have an advantage here. Arden has money and she knows how to spend it, but she doesn't know anything about getting around without it. Finally, my education in Village Estates is gonna pay off.

Pushing against her grip, I laugh.

"Let me teach you a couple things about slumming it."

# (AVIGNON)

**"This is dangerous,"** Arden says, clutching the strap of her laptop case.

Shaking my head, I ignore the exhilaration and terror running through me. I believe it when I say, "It's *fine*."

Dubious, Arden cuts me a look. But I shrug and step up to knock on the semi's door. A little while ago, I noticed somebody moving around inside, so it wasn't like I was waking the driver up. Last I looked, he was leaning back in his seat, a crossword book splayed open on the wheel.

I draw up my nerve. All this is, is asking for a ride from somebody who was fixing to drive anyway. He's sitting right there, idling and waiting. (Woulda been nice if he'd stopped whoever took our car, but no point dwelling on that.) Stepping up, I tap on the glass to get his attention.

"What?" he asks through the window.

I jerk my thumb toward the highway. "Heading west?"

Frowning, he considers me, then looks past me to take in Arden, too. Maybe I look dangerous to him. I'm the one with sharp eyes and skin tight against my skull. On the other hand, Arden is pure pixie dust, velvety soft and adorable. Like a puppy or something. Nobody's afraid of a puppy.

"My . . . uh . . . my sister and I. We need a ride."

Arden gives him the round, innocent eyes. The truck driver, though, gives Arden a look. It's one that reads loud and clear—*how exactly are we using the word sister, here?* His judgment flashes by, bright and quick. He doesn't know Arden; probably what he sees when he looks at her is skewed. He probably thinks Arden looks like a boy in girls jeggings. But for some reason, he considers her, registers his confusion, and then shrugs.

"Get in," he says.

Delighted, I drop back to the ground and hug Arden to my side. I didn't know if this would work, and the trucker's second and third looks at Arden scared the shit out of me for a second. Still, I'm gonna pretend I was sure.

"How about that?" I say.

Arden nods, her curls shivering around her face. "You're something else, boo."

It's honest, at least. And probably pretty fair. Though it feels like victory to climb into the semi, it's unnerving once we get on the road. The cab is sour with old coffee and cigarette smoke. Ashes roll off the console when we trundle over the speed bump in the parking lot. It's bigger inside than I expected, full of radios and radar detectors.

"Sit in the back," the driver says. "Ain't supposed to have anybody in here with me."

He's a thin, scraped-out man with an unshaved face. There are half-moon shadows beneath his eyes, and it's hard not to notice the way his fingers twitch against the wheel. Either he's on something, or he needs to get a hit of something.

I don't point this out to Arden because she's already queasy from the idea of *hitchhiking*.

A fuzzy little dog pops out from somewhere behind us, and I

yelp in surprise. Where did he come from? I crane around to get a look, and how about it. There's more room behind us than I realized. Instead of offering my hand for a hello sniff, I curl back to Arden. It's not that I'm afraid of dogs. It's like I said, I don't like surprises.

Still, when a trucker goes driving around with a little poof of a canine, he probably loves the thing. And if we're going to take this ride as far as it can get us, we probably ought to play nice. As the thing sniffs around my ear, I ask, "What's his name?"

"Avignon," the driver says.

It sounds familiar, but I can't place it. Arden can, though. She reads my confusion, and leans in to murmur. "It's a town in France."

"Fancy-ass name for a dog," I whisper back.

Arden shrugs. "We can all aspire."

The driver doesn't like whispering or he's bored or something. His eyes dart to the mirror, and he stares right through us. "Where you headed?"

Clutching the seat, I start lying, easily and happily. "It's hard to say. We're looking for our birth parents. See, we were adopted out, so we don't know much. Just that we're twins, and our birthday's coming up. April fifteenth, apparently. We were gonna hire a private detective, but Arden was like, let's just go try to find them."

"Twins," the trucker repeats. He frowns; his hand rests on the CB microphone. He's twitchy again, maybe thinking about calling us in or something. Fair enough, we don't look anything alike. Arden looks like somebody put her together with art in mind. I'm a tangled-up model kit, half-glued, half-painted.

"Born nine minutes apart," I say. "I'm older, but that's only because I was shoving her out of the way."

"He's bossier," Arden offers.

"Anyway," I say, "that's the two of us. How about you?"

The trucker is from Louisiana, by way of Kentucky. He doesn't have an accent that matches either place, so my guess is, he's lying too. Settling back with Arden, we listen to trucker fables and I savor the vibration of the road beneath us.

Riding in a semi isn't what I expected. The bedroom area is comfortable—there's a desk attached to the wall, a television and a computer. Everything moves, but it's like *floating*. The road bumps, and it makes a sound. The cab just sways, like it's on a cushion or something. The mattress smells like a stranger's sweat, but I guess after we leave, it'll smell like our strange sweat instead.

Arden's fingers slip into mine like they belong there. Thumb trailing along my skin, she lifts her head to ask the trucker, "Hey, can I ask you a question?"

"Shoot," he says. He glances into the mirror again, his blue eyes narrowed.

"How long would it take to drive from . . ." Arden trails off, still stroking my thumb with hers. She chose it; she reached for me. How did this happen? In a semi, with a little noodle dog bouncing all around us? It's bizarre, and I don't care. It's a sign, not from god. From Arden, that she didn't spoon me on accident, that she didn't let my hand rest on her collarbone for no reason. She took my hand; she's *holding* my hand. And she's still talking. "Let's say, Dayton to San Diego? He says four days; I think less."

"Depends. How long are you driving every day?"

"I don't know. How long would it take *you*?"

The cab fills with laughter, knowing and low. Avignon barks, a high-pitched counterpoint. "My logbooks say I drive eight hours, no more, no less. So, about four days, give or take."

My heart races, and I chase Arden's thumb right back with mine. It's a stinging, teasing touch—distracting in a good way. Curling my fingers, I shiver when Arden does too, her smooth skin slipping against mine. It's nothing, it's barely a stroke, but I'm starving for it. "Where are you stopping next?"

"Columbus," the trucker replies.

I think this is when I realize we really *are* going. This really *is* happening. It's not a walk through computer-animated forests, it's a trip through real ones. Across plains and mountains and I don't even know what else. It's the two of us, on a real adventure. There's a quest marker down the road—*find the Pearl Ship*—but the part that excites me more than finding it is getting there.

We're gonna get there. I squeeze Arden's hand tight, and right now, I could fly.

# (2491.08)

**Even though he said he was stopping in Columbus, the** trucker actually dumped us in Orient, Ohio.

The good news was, there was a buy-here-pay-here car lot sitting right there off the road. The bad news was, they took one look at Arden and her credit card, and said no. The salesman was a skinny little guy; his suit fit real nice. He probably wasn't ever gonna help us, just based on how long it took him to finally come over and ask if we needed something.

It was the credit card, though, that did it. (I wanna believe it was just the credit card; I do.) Arden showed the guy her license and everything to prove the names matched. But all of a sudden, they didn't do credit and he suggested we move on.

We thought about trying the rental place across the street, but it was more talking than actual doing. Arden said you had to be twenty-five to rent a car, and there was no way either of us was passing for that.

"I don't think we're going to get a ride out of here," Arden said as we trudged back toward the exit. Hitchhiking worked before; that was my thinking. Still, the traffic coming through here was thin, and mostly just people in work trucks. Me, I still feel guilty for letting the Mercedes get stolen. I feel guilty for dragging her out here on a quest when I didn't even think through the path.

So I'm gonna fix this. And I'm gonna do it the low-down way.

"C'mon," I say, leading her up the road where the intersection has actual stores and shit. I'm hot, I'm tired already, but we gotta get this done.

Arden carries her laptop bag with my stuff in it, slung over her neck. (That way, nobody can snatch it off her shoulder and run off with it. See? Facts you can use; Village Estates says you're welcome.) Out in muddy sunshine, this place ain't great, but it's perfect for what we need. As I march Arden toward a strip mall where a guy in a Statue of Liberty costume is waving a sign for Payday Loans, I feel like I'm Arden's tour guide into my world.

"If you wanted some beer, you could ask somebody like that," I say, pointing out the woman busking at the intersection. A cup from Burger King warms between her feet. Her cardboard sign is limp between her fingers—it claims *Two kids, lost job, please help, god bless.* Just like the *Little Dylan needs chemo* flyers. Like being poor means we've got Jesus on our side or something. Anyway. "Show 'em thirty, have 'em to go into the grocery store with half. When they come out with your beer, they keep the change and get the rest for their trouble."

"And you know this how?" Arden asks. She's not challenging me; it's like she'd be taking notes if she wasn't lugging all our crap.

I shrug. "These guys that lived down the street from me, the Cunninghams, they used to do it all the time. Gave me my first beer when I was seven."

"Bet you loved that," Arden snorts.

Shuddering, I remember the foamy warmth in my mouth, how bitter it was—how bad it tasted. And that was back before chemo ruined everything for me. But I drank the whole thing behind the maintenance shed in the complex. They gave it to me, it was mine—nobody was taking it.

"Okay, interesting," Arden says. "But how does that help us?"

"It doesn't." I smile. "Not right now, anyway. What we're looking for right now is a jackass just like Bobby."

Turning to walk backward in front of me, Arden goes ahead and asks. "Your mom's boyfriend?"

"And everybody made out of the same grease." Scanning the parking lots, I search for a familiar kind of face. Busy eyes, constantly searching. A body, constantly in motion. A shark in denim, looking for a mark or a make or a hustle. It's broad daylight, so they're a little more elusive. But I'm pretty sure if I watch one of these body shops long enough, a Bobby will appear.

It's not that mechanics are inherently dishonest—I'm not saying that at all. It's just, these guys tend to be gearheads. Look behind the wheel of a beater Trans Am, and there's a good chance you'll find a Bobby.

"Somebody like *that*," I say, catching Arden's sleeve.

There, strolling out of a muffler shop, is exactly the kind of guy I'm looking for. Expensive boots and cheap jean jacket, a lean and feral look about him as he slowly circles his car. I'm guessing it's his car, anyway. I hope he's not about to boost it.

"I don't know about this," Arden says.

With a shake, I tell her, "Trust me," then I let go. I sound braver than I am. I'm burning with adrenaline. Shit like this happens in my neighborhood all the time, but for me, it's academic.

I watched other people do this on the corner of my street. Lynne and my mother talk about guys at work pulling this kind of crap. I grew up surrounded by it. With Arden, I'm feeling ballsy enough to try it. Next to Arden, so sheltered and soft, I feel like a bandit, man. My bandit hands tremble, though.

Getting ahead of Arden, I catch the Bobby's attention first, simply by existing. Maybe I woulda been built-out if I hadn't taken a side tour through Cancerville the last couple years. Instead, I'm rangy and twitchy, and I look dishonest. That's actually a good thing, believe it or not. To a guy like this, a dirty sheen is what I need. Everything about me telegraphs: *I'm not a narc.*

Squinting, I pretend to push my hair out of my eyes as I veer closer. "Hey, do you know what time it is?"

The Bobby has a cell phone, but he looks at his watch instead.

It's gold tone and flashes—he wants me to think it's expensive. "A little past noon."

It's easy to pretend I'm distressed. My heart pounds in my chest, and a desert slowly overtakes my mouth. Knowing how people do this and actually doing it are two different things. The space between them is terrifying.

Still, I manage a convincing, "Damn it, seriously?"

The Bobby crosses his arms on the roof of the car. Leaning out long, he exposes the reptile pattern on his boots when his jeans ride up. This is where he measures me. Searches for my soft spots, tries to figure out if I'm scamming or looking to get scammed.

It makes a difference, it really does. Guys like this want to wring every last bit out of somebody. They want to borrow *your* car and *your* last two hundred dollars. Sleep it off on *your* couch and eat *your* food when you get a check from disability. But they don't want to use up *their* energy or their money or anything else.

With a Bobby, everything goes in. Ain't nothing that comes out.

Studying me intently, he says, "Afraid so. Something the matter?"

"We need to get to Cincinnati," I tell him. Finally, I gesture back at Arden. "We were making real good time on the bus, but we got off to stretch at the last stop and it left without us."

"Is that right?" the guy says. He chews, like he has an invisible toothpick in his mouth. "What's in Cincinnati?"

The sky darkens, and I almost hope it rains. I'm sweltering from the walking, but also because my body is running random symptoms by me, waiting for one to stick. I was nauseous a little bit ago, then woozy. Now it's hot flashes again and I could use a cool shower.

It would make me look even more vulnerable, counteracting Arden standing there looking like she missed the entrance to the country club. It would distract me from the blood pounding in my ears. Even from the voice in my head that laughs because *I'm a fraud, I'm a big fucking fraud*, and this Bobby is probably gonna bounce any time now.

"A job. I mean, I'm hoping, anyway. Aunt Lynne said if I could get my ass out there, she could get me on at the Waffle n' Steak."

The clouds shift, light spilling on us again. The guy looks Arden over, then straightens up. "What's your story?"

I panic. The car dealership turning us away, that rattled me and acting like I'm some white trash banger is getting to me, and I know a couple things in the world. Truck drivers with dogs named Avignon, maybe they don't give a shit when they look at Arden and see a boy wearing a lip gloss, but a Bobby does. A Bobby will beat the shit out of her just for fun; me, too, for that matter, if he knew I was queer.

So before Arden says fucking anything, I jump in.

"He can't hear you." I wave my hands around like I'm shaping words out of my flesh. I'm a dick and I know it, but I also know as far as a Bobby's concerned, Deaf and slow are the same thing. Arden being slow explains the way she's dressed; that's safer than queer. "He's Deaf. May as well just talk to me."

Arden's eyes narrow, and there's an ugly storm there. She doesn't have to say anything; I know I'm doing wrong. Then, all of a sudden, she puts on an ugly smile and raises her hand. Her thumb trails along her jaw; her palms scrape and rasp. When she curls her fingers, it's lightning fast. They dart to the same place in the air, small, then big.

I think she's signing for real, and I'm gonna have to ask her. Later. Turning away from her, I tell the guy, "He says you have a nice car."

The Bobby purses his lips, taking a step back. "You bucking for a ride or something?"

"No, no," I swear. I know I have him off balance—he can't quite get a read on us and it's making him nervous. Coming a little closer, I lower my voice. "Normally, I wouldn't ask . . . but do you know somebody who could rent a car for us?"

Looking me over slowly, the Bobby trails his fingers against his own car. Now he sees the money in it. He sees how Arden looks, and how desperate I am. Right now, he's trying to calculate how much work he's going to have to do versus how much money he's going to make. His gaze flicks toward Arden, but he asks me, "What if I could get you something clear?"

I try for innocent. "For real? That would be fucking choice. I don't have much money, though."

Right now, two things can happen. The Bobby can name a figure and make a car appear. Or he can walk away and hope something easier comes along. My skin feels like it might split, and all my insides spill out. Reason tells me that it's a Tuesday afternoon. He's probably not going to get lucky until Friday night at the earliest. Raw, naked fear says maybe I don't know dick about playing a game like this.

"What if you had five hundred dollars?" he asks, mental math registering on his face.

There's a flurry, and Arden starts to go into the bag. But no, that's too much; even for me, as bad as I am, letting Arden pay for things she shouldn't be paying for, five hundred dollars is too much. That's near a month's rent in Section 8 housing, and I don't even know what we'd get out of it. After all, this Bobby could take our money and leave us with nothing.

Conning a con man—what the hell was I thinking?

But wait. I've got something right up his alley. Oh yes, yes I do, rattling around, ready to bite. I brush Arden's hands aside and dig into the bag. Hoping that I'm not shaking too much, I lift my yellow prescription bottle just enough for this guy to see.

"What if I traded you?"

"You a cop?" he asks, suddenly.

I roll my eyes and push the bottle back down. Faking hand gestures at Arden, I say out loud, "Come on. He can't do anything for us."

The street value of honest-to-fuck oxycodone is thirty dollars a pill. Each pill. That's because I have the eighty-milligram tablets. I know this because I've listened to my mother and Lynne, up late talking. Well into the second bottle of whatever, my mother has a tendency to wander back to how expensive all this has been, and how she would have just had to *die* of cancer if it had been her. Then Lynne points out that we've got a goldmine in prescriptions.

—*This is what you do, sugar. Take one bottle, and cut all them pills in half. Give me the other half, and I know some people.*

—*Don't think I'm not tempted.*

—*Well, why not? Don't you deserve something?*

—*I figure someday, I'm gonna want to get into heaven.*

Sweating in my sheets, teeth chattering, I loved my mother so much right then. I loved her, and her pretty smile. I loved her stubby fingers and the sound of her voice. It was a sign she loved me back, at least a little. Because she told me all the time she didn't believe in heaven or hell or anything like that. Dead was dead, in her opinion. So it had to be love, even a half-moon sliver of it, that kept her from taking pain meds out of my mouth. Had to be.

But now the guy, *this* guy, this Bobby just like the one my mother was hounding for two hundred dollars, extends his arm. Holds out his hand in a "stop" gesture. "Come on, now. Nobody said that."

For two seconds, I'm victorious. I want to jump up and fist-bump Arden. But then I see the look on her face, unsettled and still.

Okay, so this is a bad thing I'm doing. I'm a bad person. I know bad things. I do bad things.

But now we have a car.

# (DRAWN BOUNDARY)

**I don't know what the silence is right now. Or quiet, I** should say. The car's loud on the highway; the radio kind of works but it buzzes. But since I paid for this ride with a handful of pills, Arden hasn't had much to say.

Now that we're on the road again, I'm starting to feel bad about the whole thing. She has a fucking Amex. Her dad *told her* to spend money on it. We should have bought bus tickets. Or train tickets. Or hell, plane tickets. So why didn't we? In the back of my head, little asshole-me knows why. Flying means the adventure is over. Buses and trains mean the adventure's not ours.

I won't cry because this is another thing that's my fault. But I want Arden back, even though I'm too afraid to reach for her hand. I think my heart might stop, for real, if she pulls away. The side of the road streaks by, flashes of tree and debris, and highway signs. Rubbing instead at the ache beneath my ribs, I roll my head to look at her. She stares straight ahead, both hands grinding against the steering wheel.

Now it feels like I have no room inside me for a breath. "Are you mad?"

"Do you *think* I'm mad?"

"I didn't know how else to get us a car!"

Sputtering, she comes to life. I just wound her key, and she's filling up the tight cab of this ancient Honda Civic with all of her Arden-ness. "Okay, that's one thing! We could have gotten on Craigslist or something and bought a beater from somebody! You'd still have all your medicine! Do you still need it? Have you been lying to me? Are you still sick?"

Rearing back in shock, I shake my head. "What? No!"

"Then why do you have them?"

"Because they're mine!" I raise my voice, even though I'm

trembling. This is the bad kind of adrenaline. It coils up, acid and green in my stomach. I used to get panic attacks in the hospital, all the time, but that was a hospital; I was supposed to feel like I was dying there. Fuck, please don't let me get a panic attack in this car, on this road, with Arden watching, fucking *please*.

Arden stares at me hard, then puts her eyes back on the road. "I don't even know what to say to that."

And like that, I feel every inch the poor white trash I've always been. Some of my problems have nothing to do with the fact that I was sick. I wish they did. It would be nice and neat that way. If I was a nice guy with a good life and happy parents, then maybe I could focus on being a miracle. I could shoot for the wounded angel thing: the strong, battle-ready human-interest story.

But you know what? I am what I am. The cancer's gone, but let's see if I'm ever really better.

This is why I should have left Arden alone. She could have kept on believing I was better. Like her. Good and selfless and innocent.

When me and Arden fought in the game, and it almost never

happened, it was just a squall. It came and went and we kept on playing. This is slow-moving, one of those tornadoes that spreads for miles and creeps along. You know it's coming; you can't do anything about it—and in the end, it destroys everything.

Arden's furious. The thumb she rubbed against mine this morning (this morning, a lifetime ago), flickers hummingbird fast against the wheel. "When this car breaks down—"

"Who said it's going to break down? It might not." I argue because I can't stop myself. "Japanese cars are immortal. They run forever."

Frustrated, Arden taps the brakes and the car jerks. "I'm just saying, *if it does*, I'm handling the next ride."

"But. You already paid for gas, and the motel. And what about your car, and—"

"Don't save me," she interrupts. "I'm not trying to save you, am I?"

Something in the dashboard pops. Icy air pours from the vents. My skin goes tight, soaking up all that delicious chill. Instead of unpacking what Arden just said to me, I convert to the air conditioner cult. Nothing matters but getting the sweat on my skin dry, the heat on my face erased. Putting both hands on the dash, I let the air sweep up my sleeves, cooling me from the inside out.

I don't know what she means. And I'm not asking, either.

# (2264)

**There's nothing but tension between us right now.**

When I lean toward Arden, I press into something physical holding us apart. A wall of static. An electric bubble. It's invisible, but real. Right now, I think touching her would be like palming a cactus.

The problem is, I know how to do all this shit, but I don't know how to feel guiltless about it. Maybe that's something you learn in the advanced class. It could be time, heat, pressure. Whatever it takes, I don't have it. Heavy with remorse, I cling to my seat belt and stare at the horizon. I already said sorry; I don't know what to do now.

"Are you hungry?" I ask.

She answers my question by way of not answering it exactly. "I thought we'd eat when we stopped for the night."

Leaning my face against the glass, I soak in the countryside. Trees and bits of city—sort of. Suburbs and shit, I guess. The highway dips and rises, sound walls and concrete blocking the view in a lot of places. When we come out of a low, deep turn, I blink.

There's the Eiffel Tower, right in the middle of Ohio. The seat belt slides through my hands and my mouth drops. It's not a mirage or an illusion, it's seriously the Eiffel Tower. Green, with an antenna on top, a single red light blinking faintly in the daylight.

Since it's not possible that we took a wrong turn and ended up in France, it has to be some attraction. One I never knew about, and I'm not sure how that happened.

"Arden, look," I say, reaching over to shake her. "Look!"

Arden leans over the wheel, her mouth turned down. "Yeah, it's King's Island."

The name sounds familiar—it's an amusement park. As we get closer, I make out the loops and whorls of rollercoasters. They fingerprint the horizon, framed by what looks like a giant water park and a whole bunch of woods. In the middle of it, *an* Eiffel Tower. Not *the*, not the one. I don't care; I never expected to see that. Seeing any Eiffel Tower is a gift.

"I've never been on a roller coaster," I tell her, twisting to take in the sight of them. They're not totally foreign. I've seen them on TV and stuff. I even saw one in person at a fair, but I was little then. Real little; all I remember is that we rode the tram, and my mother let me drink lemon shake-up out of her cup.

Slowing, melting, Arden finally looks at me again. "Everybody's been on a roller coaster."

"Not me," I say. The signs for the park flash by, pointing out parking lots and inns and restaurants all around it.

"Why not?" Arden asks.

There are lots of things I haven't done. I never went camping, or saw a concert. Never have been inside an airport, or a plane. Or a boat. Or a submarine. To be fair, she probably hasn't been in a submarine, either. Settling back, I say, "By the time I was big enough to ride, I was sick."

"Oh."

The silence stretches to the sky and back.

"Do you want to—"

"No." And without thinking, I brush my knuckles against hers. There's spark and there's heat, and—all right, I don't know why, but it's there. I think it is. (Please let that be true, *please, please, please.*)

So I do it again. It's an experimental touch—one to reassure her—one to reassure me. One that begs her to come back close again. However bad I am, I'm lonely, too. And I think, I'm just guessing, that so is Arden.

Behind the wheel, she tenses but doesn't pull away.

Softer now, I admit, "I really don't. This morning sucked, and I'm sorry, and I just wanna keep going."

The quiet this time is thoughtful. Like a miracle, Arden brushes her knuckles back against mine. "They're not that great," she says. "Roller coasters, I mean. You stand in line for a couple of hours. When it's your turn, they jam you into a seat like this big. It feels like a high chair, I'm not kidding. Because then they pull this thing over your head and it's heavy. They push it until it locks, so you can't breathe. Meanwhile, your ass is going numb. Then the train takes off and it's loud."

The stone in my belly starts to dissolve, tension ebbing away. In fact, I almost laugh, because she's just so sincere. There's more than one way to touch; she's so good with saying the right thing. Smiling at the right time.

"You're not going to convince me roller coasters suck," I tell her.

Eyes twinkling, Arden keeps a straight face. "They do. They're the worst. *Clack, clack, clack,* slower and slower all the way up the first hill. When you crest it, you pause for a split second, and I'll admit, that's pretty great. It's usually a good view of the rest of the park. But there's all this, like silent anticipation, you know?

"Then the dudebro in front of you starts screaming. Spit every-where, and *whoosh*. The whole rest of the ride, you slam against one side. You slam against the other. And you try really, really hard not to open your mouth because Spitman is spraying like a fountain."

"Are you kidding?" I ask her, getting brave and hooking my forefinger in hers. "I *love* it when strangers spit in my mouth."

Arden heaves, leaning away from me. "Sick, Dylan."

"I thought we had that in common. It's like I don't even know you. Next thing, you're going to tell me you only drink Pepsi."

She stares as if mortally offended. "You *don't*? Oh, no. This is over. You and me? Dunzo."

This is better. This is so much better. We're talking about stupid things again; we're talking again. It felt like the end of the world without her, it really did. My heart beats so fast, I'm lightheaded. It's a good feeling, *euphoric*—that one, I know how to pronounce for sure. It rolls on my tongue, sweet like candy as I lean into Arden's space again.

"Tell me," I say. "What other body fluids do you have opinions about?"

"You're gross," Arden winces. "And I went to summer camp. That's a long list."

"Start at the beginning." I tell her. "I've got nothing but time."

# (ROAD CONVERSATIONS)

**"You're smiling," Arden says.**

Brushing my fingers against my lips (because I wasn't sure I *was* smiling and wanted to check), I say, "Just thinking about future stuff. All the stuff in old science fiction is real now. Except transporters."

"I think that's on purpose," Arden muses. "You can't go on road trips if you have transporters."

"Maybe if you dialed up stops on the way," I say.

Arden drums her fingers on the wheels. "Then you could see both balls of twine in one trip."

"Stay in your weird motels. You know there's some that look like concrete tipis?"

"No way . . . wait, have you seen pictures of the Gobbler?" she asks, suddenly excited. "It was in Wisconsin; I guess it's closed now. But it was all tangerine walls and bubble windows, and shagadelic carpet and round waterbeds . . ."

I laugh. Dragging my fingers through my thin hair, I try to imagine this and fail completely. "There's an underwater hotel in Florida. It only has two rooms, though. Also shagadelic."

"Let's go there next time," Arden says.

Rolling my head to look at her, I wonder what she sees when she looks back at me. "Sounds good. Let's try not to get your car stole early on though. This scrambling for rides shit . . ."

"Sucks," she says.

"Hardcore."

How about that, though? There's going to be a next time.

# (PICK SOMETHING)

**The gas station is selling souvenir t-shirts, two for ten** dollars. I buy a pair, both extra-large. I like my clothes baggy and I don't know what size Arden is.

The shirts are soft; they smell like the cherry pipe tobacco they were sitting next to. There's a picture of an old-fashioned plane on it, and it says OHIO: BIRTHPLACE OF AVIATION. Since they printed it on preshrunk cotton, it must be true. I leave two pennies in the kitty on the counter, and head back out to the car.

"Here," I say, handing the pink tee to Arden. "I figured our jeans could go a couple days, but we needed shirts."

She unfolds her prize and spreads it on the steering wheel. With careful touches, she tugs the arms and the neck, until it's splayed out in front of her, perfectly arranged. Her whole face lights up. This is what Christmas at her house must look like, and I don't get it. It's not like she doesn't have a closet full of name-brand shit at home.

After a second, she realizes I said something. Her smile is distracted and she says, "I was thinking the same thing about underwear."

I tease, "You were thinking about my underwear?"

To my surprise, Arden blushes. Her ears turn a delicate pink, her cheeks too. It's obvious she's embarrassed by being embarrassed, because she folds the shirt up real quick and drapes it over her shoulder. She starts the car and says, "We should hit a Walmart, pick up a couple things. There's probably one around here somewhere."

"You're so weird," I tell her, pulling on my seat belt. "And I can't believe you know what a Walmart is."

"Everybody likes to save money."

When she starts the engine, I mold myself into the seat. The engine sounds smooth but there's something slightly off about the car. It runs fine, but the AC keeps going in and out. Something pings and pops under the hood every time it does. Big surprise, you don't get a quality piece of machinery for a handful of magic beans.

It makes me nervous because I want the car to last until Illinois. I'm hoping if we stop soon and let it rest, it'll do us right. It would be nice if it got us all the way to California. That's not even optimistic though. That's just stupid.

Leaving the gas station, I notice a lot of hotels on this exit. Restaurants, too, their signs starting to glow now that it's dusk. I wonder if Arden wants to stop in one of them. So far, she doesn't say much about what she wants. She doesn't make rest stops for her, but she goes every time I need to.

"Where do you want to stay tonight?" She asks *me* this, like it didn't bite her in the ass last time.

Picking up her phone, I fiddle around with the map app. "I don't care, wherever."

Dubious, she says, "Wherever. You *really* don't care."

I shrug with all the intense indifference I can muster. Arden's a mystery to me. The only way to solve her is by turning her over and examining all her edges. So I kind of want to see what she'll pick. Maybe it'll be one of those fancy hotels with room service and a guy running the elevator. Maybe it'll be another Baytes Motel.

Shifting uncomfortably, Arden pulls up to a red light. She watches it, like it might sneak a green past her if she's not paying attention. "What if I want to sleep in the car?"

"Fine by me," I say.

Rocking against the wheel, she offers, "What if we bought a tent at Walmart and camped?"

"Cool," I say. "I've never been camping."

"Hmmm."

She sounds like her dad did on the phone. It might be a bad thing to point that out, though, so I change the subject. When the light flicks green, I ask, "Are you hungry?"

With a shrug, Arden glances over. "I could eat. Where do you want to stop?"

"If you're hungry, pick something," I say.

On the phone, I zoom down to street level. All the chains are
there. Chili's and Applebee's and Ruby Tuesday, digital pushpins on a digital map. I love looking at them on the screen, then
looking up to see the real thing glide by. I defy anybody to sit
and think about it, really think about it, and not be amazed.

"I don't know, what sounds good to you?"

Leaning into her space, I clap a hand on her shoulder and peer
at her. Her profile's not as nice as the front view. Her crazy curls
cover up a lot. It looks like her brows are furrowed all the time,
like she's just walking around mad. Resting my chin on my
hand, I say, "What sounds good to *you*?"

Arden steals a look in my direction. "Is there some reason you're
messing with me, or is it just for fun?"

"I'm not, I just want you to pick."

"I really don't know," she says.

Shaking my head, I slide back to my side of the car. I always
know what I want. I even know the order I want it in. Either
Arden's lying to treat me, or she's even more alien than I

thought. Since I'm in charge of everything, I make an executive decision. "There's a Walmart. Let's just get groceries and keep going. We can drive all night."

Finally, she hesitates and admits, "I'm kind of tired."

Good enough. I'll take it.

# (LONGEST RECEIPT
I EVER SEEN)

**Three hundred dollars buys a lot at Walmart. The basket** was full; we had too much for a self-check lane.

Then the clerk called the manager, and manager called in to make sure Arden's credit card wasn't stolen. Arden was embarrassed. I was impressed. When the manager came back, he *apologized* to Arden and called her *sir*. Looking sick, Arden accepted the apology anyway.

We cart ourselves down the street, and Arden finally picks an in-between hotel. Nothing fancy with room service or anything. But nothing skanky with potential serial killers next door, either. In the lobby, they heap a plate high with fresh, free cookies. While Arden pays for the room, I snag one. Taking a bite, I sigh. It's only okay: kinda chocolate, but kinda metal. But cookies make me wonder where my old sailing buddy Coy Carmichael is tonight. If she's baking or riding away, or maybe a little of both.

When we get upstairs, I'm disappointed to realize this room has two beds. Maybe that's wrong, but I like how things ended up at the motel; all the spark and fire of accidentally touching when we were awake. All the newfound glory, waking up in somebody's arms. It was too much to hope for again, so I try to put the thought out of my head.

Arden dumps our bags on the bed by the door. She moves like she's on a mission. Spilling things out, she sorts. Crazy fast, she creates piles.

In the eating stack, all the food we bought. Apples and bananas, bread and lunch meat, mayonnaise, ketchup, mustard. Skittles. Mountain Dew. We're going to fill up the cooler we bought with ice from the hotel bins. This way, we can snack on the road and we don't have to stop unless we want to.

Next is the clothes stack, one for me, one for her. She's got a six-pack of panties; I'm guessing the same kind she always wears. I've seen the arch of them peeking over the top of her leggings, just plain, colored cotton. She pulls a bra out of the tangle, and actually stops. I'm watching her just because I like watching her, but she blushes when she realizes my eyes are on her. With a rolled shoulder, she holds up the lacy, padded lingerie and says, "It's not worth the fight at home."

"I'm sorry," I say.

She pulls the bra off the hanger and folds it neatly into her pile. Matter of fact, she looks at me and shrugs. "I mean, realistically, they're never going to be that big. Hormones get you as far as your mom's genetics will take you, and my mom's flat as a pancake."

That's new information to me, but not all that interesting to her, it looks like. It takes her all of a second to move on. The bags rustle as she rummages in them, and she starts hauling out more phat lewtz.

Next up, body stuff—toothbrushes, floss that she's gonna use but I never will. Shampoo, and I argued about that because the hotels give us shampoo. But if this is the kind that smells like her, then I guess I can use it. She smells clean to me, always. A pack of razors for her, she's got a pretty good shadow on her jaw at the moment.

Nestled in the middle of this stuff is a first-aid kit, a fire extinguisher, and an emergency roadside pack. We are *prepared*, bitches.

The last stack is dumb stuff. Bottles of bubbles and Nerf guns. Harmonicas and maracas and Koosh balls. The tiny chess set was Arden's idea. She thinks she's going to teach me to play. I've got news for her: I already know. I will kick her ass. And when I do, I will laugh and laugh.

The cookies are still warm. I press my tongue into one of the chips, soft chocolate spilling out. Waxy and sweet, it fills my mouth—it's not too bad, actually. I sprawl on the other bed because I'm supposed to act like a gentleman, even if I'm not one. Even if I'm hoping that we're going to share again, I can't just assume it. I just want all that stuff to stay over there; I want so bad for her to come over here.

"Wait, I know I bought a multitool," Arden mutters, digging around in the bags.

She's fussy, and that's funny. In the game, the way I know her best, she's undead. And it's a fact: the Forsaken are nasty. They poison everything; they leave pools of green contamination wherever they go. Their city has a canal full of toxic sludge. Their main goal in unlife is to turn the whole world into walking corpses. How do you get to be somebody who folds socks in thirds in real life, but picks an avatar that's nothing but decomp?

It makes me wonder about her, and I feel like I've done that a lot today. Rolling onto my stomach, I call her name to get her attention. When she looks, I wave my hands around with fake sign language and ask aloud, "What was that all about?"

There's a weird second where her face clouds over. But it's gone just as fast, replaced with a half smile. She replies with sweeping, elegant fingers. They wash through the air, curling, flicking. Her lips move, and then when she goes back to sorting she says, "It's ASL. I learned some at camp. One of my bunkmates was Deaf."

"For real?" I prop myself on my elbows, picking the cookie into tiny pieces. "That's cool. What do you do at camp?"

"Archery, crafts. There's usually a talent show . . ." She bounces when she finds her multitool, which turns out to be a bunch of tools all crammed together. So, now the name makes sense. She cracks it open and starts cutting tags like a champ. "Bonfires, hikes, stuff like that."

Rolling onto my back, I watch her from upside down now. She's still pretty, her hair wavering as she moves. It's a dense, dark cloud and it gets in her face—makes sense she bought another pack of hairbands.

I ask, "Was it fun?"

"No," she says. That's as direct as she's ever been, and she looks up at me like she might have to defend herself.

I break off a piece of cookie and hold it out. "Why not?"

"I started going the summer my parents got divorced." She takes the cookie and pops it into her mouth. Her hands flash again, severing tags from socks and shirts with reckless abandon. "Actually, I went to camp, and when I got home, they *were* divorced. My dad was gone."

An ache that belongs to Arden alone starts beneath my ribcage. It spreads out, taking up residence. It pushes all *my* inside soup out of the way, popping bones like toothpicks. What kind of parents do that to their kid? I thought rich people were all about mediation and talking it out and therapy and shit.

I say none of this, because I don't want her to think I'm banging on her mom and dad. I know from experience, you can call your own people assholes but the minute somebody else does it, the fight is on. So I temper my response, down to something that's focused just on her. On little baby Arden, who probably had a round baby face, to go with her round curls and her round eyes. So soft and vulnerable and woundable.

"That sucks, boo. I'm sorry."

"It's not your fault," she says.

"Doesn't mean I'm not sorry," I reply.

It's almost automatic, the way she straightens everything up. Now that everything's detagged, she starts packing again. Clothes into the backpack she picked out, food into the cooler. She organizes the world. Sorts it. Puts it in boxes. There's a tremor that runs up her back when she does it; I didn't notice that before. Her voice is even because she forces it that way.

"Mom said they were trying to make it a clean break for me. Then the next summer, *she* dropped me off at camp and Dad picked me up. So, you know, they're big on clean breaks."

There's darkness here. I see it; it casts shadows across Arden's face. It turns her mouth down, and turns the lights off in her eyes. The cookie tastes like dust now, so I put it aside. "Where . . . where did she go?"

"France. To *find* herself." A grim smile contorts her face; she doesn't look at me. She just keeps punching clothes into bags. Punishing denim instead of her family. I like to hit things when I get mad, too. "She's still there. Apparently she was *really* lost."

There's a bunch more questions I wanna ask. *Have you seen her?*

*Does she talk to you?* But I don't ask; it doesn't seem like there's a good answer waiting. Instead, I slide to the edge of the bed and reach across the gap. Arden's too far away; I can't actually touch her. I wave my hands in the air until the breeze touches her instead. "Troche-say-hey. Hey, you."

"I'm sorry," she says, trying to force her face into a smooth mask of itself. "I'm bringing you down. I'm bringing me down. Shut up, right?"

"Yeah, that's something I'd say to you never." I hold out my hand again. "Come here."

Her hesitation turns into unraveling, but she comes closer and I wrap her back up again. When her arms slip around me, I pull her head to my shoulder and pet her back in long, smooth strokes. I can't do much, but I can comfort her, you know?

I've got nothing to give her but a safe place, folded against my chest. She can hide in the curve of my neck; she's safe here beneath my hands. I'm not scamming on her; I'm not. All I wanna do right now is let her hide, and hurt, and come back out whole on the other side.

I squeeze her tight and I murmur, "People just suck sometimes. They don't think about anybody but themselves."

"Yeah, I know."

Her breath seeps through my shirt, marking me red hot. For a minute, she lets herself disappear in me. But just a minute; it's almost like she can't let herself relax. When she starts to give in she pulls away. There's light between us, then she steps back. She swallows hard, then takes a deep breath.

To give her some privacy, I look away because she's trying to put herself back together. I get that. When her breath falls even again, I tug on the hem of her shirt. I dip my head to catch her eyes, because she's still staring at the floor.

I promise her, "I'll be the one who stays."

The air in the room suddenly clears. It's clean and sharp, so thin everything looks brighter. That's the first time I'm not afraid of where I'm going. Destination, mostly unknown. Normal unknown, life, unknown, but one thing's for sure.

When it comes to Arden, I'll be the one who stays.

# (NIGHTSWIMMING)

**I slide out of sleep like I'm slicked with oil. Greasy sweat** trails fire along my skin. The bed lurches beneath me, or maybe I arch off of it.

Peeling Arden's arm from my waist, I slip from the bed and stagger toward the bathroom. Nothing makes sense at first. The geometry of the room is off, with corners doubled up and the floor at an angle. One of the lights buzzes and it casts a greenish haze—maybe I'm just seeing greenish.

Splashing cold water on my face, I wait for a wave of nausea. I don't know why I'm sick, I just know it's coming. It's gonna hit any minute. This isn't chemo sick. This isn't even detox sick, and fuck, I don't miss that at all.

Snatches of dreams waver just at the edge of my thoughts. I was inside an MRI again; it clanged, something was wrong—the more I try to remember what happened, the worse it makes me feel. It doesn't seem fair that a light show that your brain puts on when you're unconscious should have any kind of power, but it does.

It woke me up, but it's got claws in. It's turning bad dreams into anxiety, making it flutter in my chest and twist in my gut. I lean over the toilet for a long time, but nothing happens. Nothing comes up, and finally I give up. I rinse my mouth and stumble from the bathroom. I bump the bed, then lean away from it. As if it's the bed's fault I had anxiety dreams—*yeah, blame the mattress and the pillows that actually fluff, Dylan, do that.*

I snatch the key card from the dresser and wobble to the door. I don't want to be sick like this when Arden's in the room. For a long time, the doctors had me on pills to help the anxiety. Funny thing was, they didn't help a lot—you can't chemical away being scared of dying when you're dying, it turns out. Now, though, I sort of wish I had them. I'm scared for no reason, and I feel helpless. If she wakes up, she'll feel helpless, too.

I gotta get out of here. Just long enough to get my head back. Just long enough to get some air. I fling myself out of the room.

The hall is too long and too tall, stretching like a cathedral above me. Chlorine stains the air, and I follow the smell. It seems like swimming would help, if I could just cool off. Get the sweat off me, and float a little bit. My mouth hangs open, spit pooling. I don't want to swallow; it tastes like chewing foil, like licking batteries.

Pulling my shirt to my mouth, I spit into a fold of it and sway against the wall. It holds me up and I walk and walk and walk. Forever, it seems like. The walk from my bedroom to the kitchen is forever at night. Even when my mother craps out in front of the TV, and I have three a.m. infomercials lighting the way, it's so far.

At the end of the hall, I stare at myself. All my molecules screech to a halt and I whimper. I'm a ghost, pale and transparent. Tipping my head one way, then the other, I approach myself. Did I die? I really want to know, because this is some cartoonish bullshit, being out of my body and seeing myself from a distance. Creeping closer, I hold my breath. It raises an unsteady hand; I do too.

Then I crash into a glass wall. Found the pool.

My key card opens the glass door. A humid curtain sweeps over me. Chlorine burns my nose. Wavering blue crescents decorate the walls, the ceiling. The lights are out, the only illumination coming from beneath the water. I leave the card on a frosted glass table and walk to the edge of the pool. All I wanna do is cool off. I just need to get wet and get my shit together, that's all.

My head is a dizzy, twisted mess. Innately, I know I probably don't have the coordination to swim right now. Shallow end, though, I can walk in the shallow end.

Grabbing the rail, I take the first step. Lukewarm water rises up my ankles, my shins. It's a kiss, swallowing me up as I sink deeper. To my knees, to my hips. Though I'm unsteady, the waves push me upright again. Or maybe it's the opposite of that. I don't know. I just don't know, and I start to cry.

I cling to the edge, my hands scrabbling until they catch hold. Finally steady, I close my eyes and hold on. The current pulls my shirt one direction but darts beneath it in another. It's so good, a cool caress to wash all the sick away. My belly hitches. Salt down my throat, chemicals in my mouth, I choke through a sob and will it all to stop. Just stop.

Leaning my head back, I don't care that my pillow is concrete. That my clothes are soaked. That I don't have a towel. I don't care because my head is clearing.

Sinking beneath the surface, I listen to the low, distant sounds of an empty pool after dark. My hair wavers around my face. It tickles, streaking in the light.

This would be a good way to die, maybe. A better way to go, one that I chose. I could hold on to something heavy and just let the flood come. Fill me up, drag me down, it doesn't take that long. I think only a couple of minutes, as long as the water isn't subzero.

Except *miracle*, bitches, I'm *better*. Maybe drowning woulda been a good way to go before now, but my lizard brain is *not* okay with it now. Not even a little. I surface. I breathe. The sound of my gasp echoes on, buffeted by the waves, repeated against the tile and glass. I'm better, I'm fucking better. That's the thought that finally pushes the dream and the anxiety down to rest.

Slowly, I drag myself out of the pool. I'm dripping everywhere and couldn't care less. Leaden feet and heavy shoulders, I scrape the key card off the table. Then I stand there, drawing in, draining out. The blue lights shimmy around me. Artificial galaxies, stirred up by my existence.

I grab one of the abrasive white towels by the door and drape it over my head. Our room isn't so far down the hall as it was before. Now I notice the real world. The pizza box outside room 135; the laughter behind door 115. Then, the soft sigh Arden makes when I slip into 104 again. Though I close the door quietly, she turns toward the sound.

Leaning against the door, I catch my breath again and plan. I'll dry off and eat half a banana. No pills. I won't take any pills, but I'll drink some water and climb back into bed. With Arden's arm pulled over my waist again, I'm going to sleep so good.

Better than I have in days, because I realized something back there in the pool: I'm not gonna die. Yeah, I got better, but that's not why. I'm not gonna die because I just decided I don't want to anymore.

# (OTW BRT)

**While Arden packs the car, I claim the keys. It's been a** couple days since I drove, and I'm tired of just riding. Plus, secretly, I can admit this to you—I want to make sure we get back on 70 after Indianapolis. Because of the trucker, we got shunted down to 71 to Cincinnati. It was a detour, and a pretty good one, since I got to see the Eiffel Tower.

But we gotta get this quest back on track. Back the way it should be. 70's just a good route. Straight through the middle of the country. Not too north, not too south. There's stuff to see on the way: the Mississippi River, the St. Louis Arch, canyons and mountains and a whole bunch of states I've never been to. Tunnels. Snow in the springtime—I think there is, in Vail. You get to Utah and you turn left, it's that easy.

It's something to be sure of; something I can hold on to. This is the road that takes me all the way to the Salton Sea. *This* one. No other. Relaxing in the driver's seat, I flash a big smile at Arden when she comes to the door.

"Kick back," I tell her. "You were talking in your sleep last night."

She hems a little, shifting uncomfortably. It's kind of obvious she wants to be behind the wheel, but today, I want to drive. And like before, Arden doesn't want to push it. She rubs her hands against the sill of the window, her eyes darting from me, to the distance. "I really don't mind driving."

"Me either," I say.

"I know, but . . ." She trails off. I see her struggling.

I cover her hands with mine and peer up at her. This morning, there's a new shade of green in her eyes. I didn't notice it before; it's almost golden, feathery streaks of it between the darker strands. She has the prettiest eyelashes. They're long and curled and I'm staring way too much at her face. I was in the middle of a thought, so I get back to it. "C'mon, Arden. Please?"

She hates herself. I see it flash across her face as she pushes off the door. She's giving in, against her better judgment, and I feel almost bad for her. I'd feel worse, except I really *do* want to drive. When she slides into the passenger seat, I tip to one side.

Resting my head briefly on her shoulder, I say, "Thank you."

"Just be careful."

"I will. You look out for cool stuff," I reply, and we're off.

Too bad for me, it's a pretty dull piece of highway. Trees billow up again, blotting out any towns that might be on the side of the road. There's a weigh station and I consider pulling into it. It's for trucks only, but what are they going to do, arrest me? Illegal weighing? What if I told them I was having a seizure and I *had* to pull over?

"Do you smell chlorine?" Arden asks.

Soaking up the rumble of the engine, I shrug. "Like I said. You were talking in your sleep, so I went to the pool. It was dark down there, it was pretty cool."

"You should have woken me up."

I feel bad, because she says it like she missed something

completely amazing. Pressing a hand to my chest, I swear to her, "The darkness was cool, but the water was warm. Too many chemicals. I basically walked in and walked right back out."

"Walk in, walk out, huh? Just like that time we thought we were going to clear Blackwing Lair, just the two of us?" Her grin spreads easily, her eyes crinkling at the corners.

Blackwing Lair is a dungeon in Warcraft, one of the old-world ones. Which means nothing to you (unless you play, in which case, stop by and say hey sometime. We play in the Uldum realm, usually like, nine to midnight, eastern time zone. Go Horde or go home.), but it means a lot to us. Anyway, like I said before, if you're not in a guild on the game—a raiding club, more or less—you never get to see the really cool stuff on the regular.

So what we do is wait until we outlevel it. Blackwing Lair was hardcore raiding when the game only went to sixty levels. It took forty people to finish it. Now that we're both level 100, Arden and I can waltz through the place, the two of us alone. The first time we went, though, we were 70 and—like the pool—we walked in and walked right back out.

Arden barks a laugh, reaching over to shake me. "You remember when my keyboard went crazy and—"

"You were typing like, in Klingon," I finish with my own laugh. "That was the same night that Death Knight froze that pool we were jumping in."

With a groan, Arden shakes her head. "That was only funny for you. I'm the one who died."

We spill our own history, and it makes magic, here and now. In a Honda Civic, on a stretch of highway that leads to the Salton Sea. It may be imaginary history we share, but it's real enough. It's threaded with real memories, even if the world was programmed and put online.

One night, we went to take the scam ride to the top of the Twin Colossals. The forest around us was lush and green. The zone was quiet because nobody went to Ferelas unless they had to. It was out of the way, and the only dungeon there was overpowered. And by then, all the loot in it was obsolete. It was good for a walkthrough if you wanted to see it. That was about it.

Mostly, I remember it, because that was the night Arden told me about losing her virginity.

"It was slightly damp," she'd said. "Smelled like Deep Woods

Off. Lasted about as long as a black banana."

Now that I know more about her, I think I know exactly where it happened. At that camp. The thought distracts me. Am I right? All of a sudden, I *need* to know, like I need water and sun and air. Beneath my hands, the wheel buzzes. This car is even weirder to drive than it is to ride in. The dashboard abruptly ping-pops, and here comes the AC.

With a frigid breeze on my face, I glance at Arden. "Was your first time at summer camp?"

"Huh? What the what?" Arden asks. "Where did that come from?" She's not mad; she's confused. I don't blame her, the question came out of nowhere.

"I was just thinking about it—"

"Well, that's unnerving."

"I know," I say, nudging her. "Was it?"

Busying herself with the bag at her feet, Arden shrugs. "Yeah, why?"

"You said you hated camp," I point out.

"It had its moments," she replies. She pulls a headband from the bag and slides it on over her eyes like a visor, then up. It smooths her hair from her face, a wild cascade of curls puffing up behind it. And you know what? It shows off how pretty she is. How clear and unmarked her skin is. The soft, expressive pinkness of her lips.

I'm staring at her, and I only realize it when she bugs her eyes at me. "What?"

"You did the nasty in a bunk bed."

Now she laughs and nudges me back. "Shut up."

"Was it a guy?" I ask suddenly. And then I want to take the words and stuff them back into my mouth. Because I don't want to know, and I do.

A blue sign welcomes us to Indiana; we're coming up on Batesville, the casket capital of the world. We're just fifteen miles away!

I don't believe we'll be visiting, thanks.

"It was a girl," Arden says, and I guess she knows that makes me wonder about stuff she doesn't want to think about, because she challenges me: "Where did you lose yours?"

"In a water bed," I reply. This is technically true. It was a hydro-therapy bed in the hospital. The heat was turned up way too high, but those rooms were dark. They piped in music, and we could lock the doors. André was sicker than I was, and he believed in bucket lists.

Now it's her turn to be nosy. "And it was a guy, right?"

I nod. A guy, who's dead, and suddenly . . . I miss him. We weren't even together, really. We were just hospital friends and it was a last chance. I feel his ghost slip between my fingers, whisper against my lips.

"Water beds are creepy," Arden says, moving along. "Like vans."

"Are you *judging* me? You did it in a bunk bed!" Needling her, I laugh. "On the top or the bottom? Tell me. Tell me right now, bunk baby!"

But before she can, a siren cuts through the air. This time, I'm the one who hits the brakes; I can't help it. The siren's so loud because it's close. Right on our ass. And when I look in the rearview mirror, I realize the lights are going and the cop is pointing at the side of the road. Pointing at me.

Of course. This is my fault too. I tempted the universe when I promised everything would be fine.

# (WARNING)

**"Shit, shit, shit," I say, pulling off.**

I cut the engine and roll the window down. Splaying my empty hands on the windowsill, I wait for the cop to walk up and bust us. The problem with buying cars with drugs (besides the fact that you bought a car with drugs) is that you don't know for a fact that the car's legit. It could be stolen. The plates could be stolen. I have insurance and I know there are no bodies in the trunk, but otherwise, this is a disaster.

Beside me, Arden quietly hyperventilates. Her lips barely move as she murmurs to me, "My dad is going to kill me. With his bare hands. He will. When I was little, that's how he kept me in line. He'd say, 'If you make me come after you, you *will* regret it.'"

"No offense, but your dad is a dick," I mumble back, watching the rearview mirror. Fumbling with my bag, I pull out my license. I got my license right after I lost all my hair for the second time, and I don't know why, but at this particular moment, I think that's funny as hell. I flash the picture at Arden, like *check it out, I look like an egg.*

She smiles weakly and retrieves what little paperwork there is in the glove box. She's not shaking; she's just tense and pale as she hands it over.

The cop finally climbs out of her cruiser. I watch her in the mirror—she waits for a semi to pass to start this way. It seems like it takes her forever to walk up to our car. Her gun belt sets her off balance. Her hips sway, but she's not unsnapping the holster, so that's good. That is a motherfucking relief, right there. Chances are, we're not getting shot today. Woo hoo.

"Morning," the officer says, leaning down to peer at me. "Got your license and registration?"

I'm gonna puke in my lap. What if that Bobby reported this car stolen? What if that son of a bitch took my drugs and then decided he wanted takesie-backsies. Guys like that, you never know. You just never fucking know. Gathering my thoughts, I hand everything over and say, "I'm really sorry; I don't know what I did."

Brows knitting, the cop looks over my license. She flips it on the back side, then on the front again. Clipping it to her ticket board, she holds it close to her body, protective. She doesn't need to, I swear to god, the last thing I'm trying to do right now is snatch my license and flee the scene.

Stepping away, she touches the mic on her shoulder and reads something off my paperwork. Then she waits, occasionally cutting a look in my direction. Finally, a crackly voice responds. I can't tell dick from what it's saying. It could be *Arrest this brat on sight; his mother wants to know where the hell her car is and the DEA wants to have a little sit-down.*

Whatever it was, the cop's nostrils flare and she leans into the window. It takes me a second to realize she's sniffing the air in the car. Looking at my eyes.

"Speed limit through here is seventy," she says. "Any particular reason why you were going fifty?"

Shock floods me. Not too fast. Not broken taillight. Not stolen plates—holy shit, she thinks I've been toking! Which kinda pisses me off, actually. Mom and Lynne used to buy this bunk shit from some guy Lynne knew. He gave it to her cheap because it was supposed to be for Little Dylan Needs Help God Bless, but hell no. They smoked that shit. I just smelled it through the vent.

I sit there like an idiot for a minute, then realize the cop wants me to say something now. I spit out the first thing that comes to mind; it's not even true. "I get scared on the highway."

With a step back, the cop leans down more completely. Her head and her hat fill the entire window. Her eyes narrow; she stares right into me. It's like she's trying to snake charm me. All it does is stir up the panic inside. I feel like I can't get a breath, not a good one. And I'm afraid to try, because what if breathing deep makes me look guilty?

"Then why are you driving on it?"

"For practice," I say. Tears suddenly spill down my cheeks, and it's so fucking embarrassing. It's not on purpose; it's like everything else. Was I stronger when I was little? Is this something that happened to me? Or would I have been like this no matter what?

I try hard to suck it up. I don't want the cop to get pissed, but I've read stories too. People like us getting pulled over and they're never seen again. Seems like my whole life, the only time the cops come around, they make shit worse. So, just like with the Bobby, I edit and try to talk fast to get us out of here. "There wasn't a lot of traffic, and it's an easy drive, Arden said he would take over if I got too scared. I'm really sorry."

The officer looks to Arden. "Let me see your license."

All of a sudden, Arden's frown deepens. We exchange a look, but she pulls out her license and hands it over. I can't help but steal a look at the picture. Her hair's in a jock cut, and she's wearing a blue polo shirt. There's just this air around her, like she just got done robbing Ralph Lauren for blow money and she's dead inside.

We both watch as the cop wanders back to the back of our car. Now she's making another call in her shoulder mic and time stretches out forever. Her face is a flat, neutral mask. She could be thinking anything.

If she strides back to her cruiser, we're screwed. Going back there means she needs to get something important. A ticket printer, or handcuffs, or who the fuck even knows what. Nothing good, so she needs to just stay where she is. Everything will be okay if she does. I believe this. It's a mantra now, stay here, just stay here. Arden vibrates beside me. She's a tuning fork, singing in the key of *we're fucked*.

The oracle of the cop's shoulder mic bursts to life again. For a long time she stands there, talking back and forth. Then, her mask slips a little. She rolls her eyes a little; shakes her head. Then she walks back to my window. Reaching past me, she returns Arden's license. Then she unclips mine, but holds on to it firmly.

"Everybody's gotta learn sometime. But if you can't keep up with the flow of traffic, let your boyfriend drive."

With a flick of her fingers, she thrusts my license and the registration at me. So grateful, I clutch it. Then I all but tumble out of the car to switch places with Arden. Wary, the cop backs up. When she realizes that I'm just doing what she told me to, she continues to back toward her car, but slowly. Watchfully.

Arden slides over, and she's already adjusting the mirrors when I get back in. Before I say a word, she turns to me. "We have to get rid of this thing."

"Yeah, we do."

There's this intense edge to the silence. When Arden hits the gas, we rocket back onto the highway, right in front of the cop. Grabbing the Jesus strap above the window, I hold on tight. I don't know if she's trying to drive opposite of the way I was, or what. But she's scaring the shit out of me.

Then, like clockwork—just like her, she rides the brakes. For a second, I'm afraid we're gonna flip into the culvert. Maybe roll over a couple of times, die down in a ditch on the wrong high-way, because we're on the wrong highway. I don't know why that fact buzzes in my ears, but it does. This is I-74; if I have to check out now, I don't want it to be on I-74.

"I'm going to say something," Arden informs me. Her voice is mercury, spilling and slipping unexpectedly. "Because I didn't last time; this is going to be the last time."

Oh shit. I push myself back in the seat and look at her. All I say is "Okay."

Hands tight on the wheel, she whips back into the slow lane. Her jaw is tight and set, and she doesn't look at me, not at all. "I don't know if you have a problem with it, or if I'm getting too confusing for you or what, but I'm not a guy. I'm not ashamed of who I am. And I'm not going to drive all the way to California with you if that's an issue."

Stunned, I gape. "I . . . what? Arden, what the hell are you talking about?"

"You've done it twice," she says. She holds up two fingers and waves them at me. "When we bought the car, and just now."

I don't know what *it* is. I swear to god, I don't, except then my

Swiss-cheese brain kicks in. A hot, defensive blush burns up my throat. "I know who you are, boo! I was just trying to protect you!"

"Yeah, that's what my dad says, too."

And I take it back. I take it all back, when she says that—when this beautiful girl who wouldn't even pick a fucking McDonald's for herself says that—I change my mind.

I do want to die on I-74. Right here. Right now.

# (2213.04)

**The world flattens, and there's nothing. Nothing to look** at. Nothing to point out to start a conversation. Nothing to look forward to, except getting back on 70 at the other side of the city.

Spindly trees threaten to bloom but haven't yet. There's some green on the side of the road, but mostly, it's leftover winter here. Everything's dirty and deserted. Trash gathers on barbed-wire fences; the paint peels on billboards that only advertise the fact that you can advertise on the billboard.

Asphalt hums beneath the tires and I'm starting to wonder why that cop even pulled us over. This road is so smooth, so straight, I could drive it in my sleep. There's barely even traffic on it.

Arden, though, drives it like it's a demolition derby. Her knuckles are almost white on the wheel, she's gripping it so hard. She's wound tight, her jaw fixed and her lips flat and pale. For once, she doesn't ride the brake and that's not even a gift right now. It's a sign, one I read too late.

Everything under my skin is thrashing; I feel like a bag of snakes. I coil and uncoil against the door as I stare at spindly trees and empty fields. For a while, I hate that cop. It's her fault any of this came up. Who gives a shit if somebody's driving too slow? Almost, I convince myself she was trying to explode this quest.

I don't wanna be mad at Arden either, but I am, kind of. How come I don't get credit for intentions? Why doesn't it matter that I was trying to help?

Arden's phone rings. We exchange a look, but she picks it up to answer. As soon as she hears the hello on the other line, I know who it is. It was possible for her to get stiffer, and she did. Her voice is measured, and she puts on this grimace. It's like she's trying to smile, trying to get the sound of it in her words.

"Yeah," she says, tapping the brakes. "We're making good time. Should be there by ten, I think?"

Her lies aren't even heavy. She doesn't stop to think, or look panicked or anything. If anything, she's tired. Bored. She feeds him some bullshit about stopping at the border to New York for lunch. We'd probably be a lot closer, except there was traffic backed up a long time, and *then* we left my phone at a gas station. Lost a half an hour doubling back for it. Yeah, I'll be keeping a better eye on that in the future, ha-ha-ha.

In this world Arden just made up for Concrete Blocks, we're heading up to Caroga Lake for the week. I have a lake house in the Adirondacks; we're meeting my cousins up there. It's gonna be a good time.

Arden hits the brakes again, but this time to slow down. Suddenly, we have signs—suddenly, there's a city jutting up out of nowhere. It's like somebody swept the landscape clean, then dropped Indianapolis smack in the middle of it.

"Yes sir," she says flatly, changing lanes once, and then back. The directions are kind of confusing here. Go this way, and the road ends, that way, you end up on an interchange loop. All kinds of interconnected lines on the map are accounted for, 74 and 70, east and west, 465 north and south, 65, 31 . . . jesus christ.

Since Arden has her phone, all I have is the map in my head.

It's not good for this kind of driving; I know points—place to place—but the details, they're fuzzy. When I think I've figured out the way, I point at the sign, then at the right lane.

For the first time in over an hour, Arden acknowledges me. She nods, faintly, and follows my directions. Shifting the phone from one ear to the other, she summons that twisted smile again. It comes out with a dry laugh. "As far as I know, nobody's bringing beer. But if somebody *did*, I promise none of us are driving."

And there's Concrete Blocks, surprising me again. All things being equal, if I hadn't ever been sick, my mother would probably party with my friends. She'd buy the beer, and I don't even wanna think about that in detail.

But there's Concrete Blocks, stick in the ass, leaves strangers standing in front of his open door, Concrete Blocks being all *understanding*. Knowing a spring break trip away from home is probably about boozing; only being worried that Arden doesn't get hurt doing it.

He's just trying to protect her.

The venom in me turns to foam. It fizzes in my veins; I slump in my seat. Arden's not wrong about me. It wasn't the cop that fucked things up here. It wasn't the Bobby; it was probably only half the fact that I bought a car with drugs. She said it then, too. I remember it now: I blew past it at the time, I asked if she was mad about the drugs and she was like, "Okay, that's *one* thing."

There was the other thing. This thing.

It's easy to orbit around her in the game, and remember who she is, and get it right. We're both chicks in the game, but more importantly, we're not even human. Outside of the game, even, I know Arden's a girl. I don't doubt that; it's not like it's an opinion or anything. It's a fact: Arden is a girl and always has been.

Just the same; I'm gay and I always have been. I was gay when I was little Dylan, and I was gay when André marked me off his bucket list, and I'm gay now, wanting to hold Arden's hand and lay next to her in the hotel and get her to look at me again. Or did I change? Am I bi or something? Or am I a dick who says the right words, but thinks the wrong things?

I lied about who she was twice, twice when it was easier, and yeah, I thought I was doing it for the right reason, but shit. I'm just like her dad.

No, I'm worse than her dad, because I know better.

# (CHAPTER WESTERN INDIANA)

**All the way on the other side of the city and burning day-**light toward Illinois, Arden speaks again.

"Do you have a boyfriend?"

It's a question that has nothing to do with anything. It's literally out of fucking nowhere, but I cling to it. I grab for it, like it's the last roll on the table, like it's water in the desert. I need the sound of her voice and I'm going to scrabble for all I can get. I don't care that there's no context; I don't care that it's dangerous.

I say, "Where would I get a boyfriend?"

She shrugs. "I don't know, the internet?"

Just the thought of that makes me laugh. It's not like I don't know about shit like Tinder and Grindr and why don't they just call them Fuckr, that's what I wanna know. But I'm underage, have a body by Frankenstein, and I live with my mother. Nobody in their right mind wants to hook up with that.

I twist into the backseat to grab a snack, a treat—I find a bag of Skittles. I pull them into my lap and assure Arden, "Nobody put a ring on this, go figure."

"Unbelievable," she says. A light—a smile! It starts soft at the corner of her mouth, but it lingers.

It's my turn to talk, and I realize, I don't even know which way she goes. In my head, I guess I figured she's a girl, she's into guys—but that was before I knew about what she did in the camp bunk beds. "What about you?"

I tear open a bag of Skittles, spilling them into my lap to sort. Arden says she wants the purple ones first, then the red ones. They smell good to me, but I know if I pop one in my mouth, it'll just taste like fruity chemicals. Starburst, too. SweeTarts. Man, I used to love SweeTarts, the big ones that are chewy.

Reaching over because I'm not sorting fast enough, Arden grabs a couple to get started. "No. I mean, I was kind of seeing a guy last summer, but it was just . . ."

The candy clicks against her teeth. She's not chewing it, she's sucking it. Arden does things all wrong. She puts ice in her coffee and throws the top bun off her hamburgers. She's the kind of gorgeous that makes girls stop and say *daaaaaamn* under their breaths when she walks by. I know; I heard two girls in the Walmart do it.

"Bad?" I offer.

She looks thoughtful. "A bad fit."

"Nothing since then?"

"There's nobody I want to hang out with at my school," she says. Her lips are lined purple, distractingly dark. "Mona tried to set me up with one of her friend's nieces but it was just awkward."

Intensely curious, I speed my sorting because I want to watch her face. Emotions cascade over it. They leap from brow to lash, to lips, to eyes. She's got so much expression going on, I could stare at her for hours. "Was she a dog or something?"

"No, she was nice," she says, and I think she probably means it. "Bisexual, chill about me, you know. Zero chemistry, though. She's into jocks, I'm into . . ."

"Giant cows," I joke. My character in the game, in case you forgot.

"With their big brown eyes," Arden says wistfully, then breaks into a new smile. "I don't know, maybe. You're more fun to look at in real life, though."

Rolling my eyes, I try to play off the blush. I try to hide everything buzzing down in my chest. She's flirting with me, right? She is—I don't think she just got over being mad; instead, she moved on, and this is what we do in the game, right? This is what we're good at. I swallow the knot in my throat before I reply; I don't want my voice cracking in front of her. "Whatever, whatever."

"Dylan," she says. "You all right?"

Even though I know it'll end badly, I pop a couple of lemon Skittles into my mouth. Ugh, oh god, it's like chewing furniture polish. My mother sprays Pledge in the house when we have visitors. It smells classier than air freshener, she claims. Because people can't look around at our prefabricated bullshit furniture and figure out we haven't been having the maid in to polish the antiques.

With a deep breath, I look to her. "I'm sorry," I say. "About before."

The mood hazes, just for a second. Then Arden says, "Don't be sorry. Just don't do it again."

Because she's gracious, I'm ashamed. For doing it, for trying to put the blame on her or the cop or anybody but me. I'm pretty bad at this, I have to admit. I suck at being next to her in the real world. Makes me wish for pixels.

Arden clears her throat. "So anyway . . ."

"I do like this one chick," I say suddenly. I suck down a half a bottle of water and finish the thought. "Purple hair. Huge glowing yellow eyes—she keeps me up all night."

"Lucky girl."

"Yeah, I know," I say with a thin laugh. I gesture at my every-thing: my weedy, knotty body. "She's getting allllllll dis."

"I'll steal you away," Arden says. "You wanna get married?"

To my surprise, I don't stammer. I don't stumble; I look at her and it's easy. "Well yeah, but I don't even know if you're pan or bi or what."

Softly, all her lights turning back on inside, Arden says, "I'm everything. I'm the whole world."

# (RED SKY)

**I drum on the dashboard, wearing myself out. All of a** sudden, I have this nervous energy that I have got to get out. It rumbles and buzzes. I'm all alive for no reason at all, except we're heading west and the sun follows us with every mile.

Turning to Arden, I squeeze her hand. "You ever been to California?"

"Yeah," she says. Her concentration drifts away, like she's trying to frame a memory or something. It comes back, sharp and bright. Her eyes are so green. "Yeah, with my mom and dad. They left me with my grandmother, and they went to Napa. A wine-tasting tour or something like that."

"Boring," I say, dropping into my seat. "What did you do while they were boozing it up?"

Arden shakes her head. "Not much. There were—wait. Oh yeah! Oh my god. I totally forgot this!"

"What?"

Arden leans forward. She talks a little slow, like she's not sure about her own memories. "There were . . . there were wildfires when we were out there. In the mountains."

Now that's something I never thought about. Like, for me, tornadoes are a real thing. Blizzards, too. Occasionally hurricanes. But wildfires? That's something exotic. I could try to picture it, but instead I crowd into Arden's space. Squeeze it out of her squishy memory.

"What did it look like?"

A strange smile spreads across her face. " I went outside to get the mail, right? And everything was red. It was like I was on Mars."

"The hell?"

"That's what it looked like," she exclaims. Her words tumble out, rolling over each other. "Red. Like, the sky was red, and the sun was up there. Glowing, through the haze, it looked like another sun from another planet. Here's the weirdest part, though. I tried to take pictures of it, but they all came out normal."

I squinch my eyes at her. Is she yanking my chain? Arden jokes, but she doesn't usually make shit up just to see if I'll believe it. That's one of the nice things about spending my nights with her, in person or in the game. She's stand-up. I don't have to worry about her getting a rise out of me just for giggles. "Normal how?"

Arden checks her mirrors, changes lanes, then looks back at me. "It was my dad's old camera, a pretty good one. It's got all these auto-correct settings on it, and I guess it saw red sky and was like, nope. Shift that back to blue. I tried it with my phone, too, and nothing. When we got home, my dad was like, what the hell did you take so many pictures of nothing for?"

Protective of Arden, even in a past tense where it's all done and all gone, I tense. "Did you tell him? Did you explain?"

Her smile fades, then shifts. It's more rueful now. Quiet. "No. They didn't come out, so what was the point?"

"Yeah, but it wasn't your fault," I say stridently.

"It could have been."

If I poke her, then I'm as bad as her dad. But I want to poke a little bit, because she's got to have some pride in there somewhere. The only thing I've managed to accomplish so far in my life is almost getting arrested for sailing down a culvert in a pool, kidnapping Arden from suburbia, and walking out of a high school admissions office because I was too embarrassed to explain my mother wasn't ever gonna come down there. Despite all that, everything wrong with me, I think I like my dumb ass more than Arden likes herself. And that makes me crazy, because she's amazing.

The quiet goes on long enough that Arden peers at me. "What?"

"You know what?" I tell her. "We get to California, this time? We'll find my ship. And then we're gonna find some fires for you to take pictures of."

Arden takes her hand back and my heart sinks. But then, she rubs her palm dry on her leggings. Then she takes my hand again, lacing our fingers together. Gently, she brushes our joined touch against her cheek, so soft—so sweet. I like that she did it out of the blue; from the shade of pink crossing the bridge of her nose, I think she likes it too.

"What if there are no fires when we get there?" she asks.

I shrug. This one's easy. "Then we'll set some."

# (REST)

**We passed the casket capital of the world, drove right** through the Crossroads of America. Now we're cutting through scrubby, smooth Illinois, at least the southern tip of it. Chicago livens up the state, but that's 200-something miles north of here.

Arden claps my shoulder with the back of her hand. "Rest stop!"

Then, she yanks the wheel so hard, the car shudders as it veers. As happy as I am that she decided to take a stop for herself, it would be nice if she didn't try to scare the shit out of me at the same time. We cut down the road marked CARS, and she glides into a spot. Bounding out of the car, she leaves me in the dust.

I don't have to go or anything, but the longer I sit there, the better a walk-around sounds. I ache from sitting, and I'm trying to place exactly where we are. There's something good coming up in Illinois, something Arden has to see. I don't want to tip her to it, but I want to make sure we don't accidentally blow past it either. There's probably brochures in the rest stop.

Yeah, time to get up. Time to move.

Unfolding my legs, I climb out of the car. Humidity coils around me, and that sucks. But it smells like there's rain coming. I turn, searching. Then I find a silver maple and nod to myself. Its leaves are turned over. All of them, cloaking the tree in ghostly green instead of a deeper shade. That tree knows that rain is coming too.

Inside, just like I thought, there are brochures. About sixty million things to see in Illinois, but I shake my head. Half of them are on highways far away from here. A few more, they're just restaurants and hotels, nothing special. Some caves, it looks like, but the last thing I want is to put myself down in the ground. I just don't.

When I don't see what I'm looking for, I turn my attention to the map on the wall. Walking my fingers across it, I find the red dot that represents where we are. Then I splay my touch along the line and stop. I smile; Vandalia, Illinois—we're not there yet. Tucking that fact in, all warm and safe against my chest, I head outside.

There's a wall of vending machines around the side, so I go and take a look. I don't want anything in particular, just to move. Get some blood back in my hands and feet. As I step into the kiosk, the red glow of a Coca Cola machine greets me. There's a hot drink machine next to it, which makes my stomach turn. When I first got sick, me and mom spent a lot of nights in the emergency room, drinking fake chicken broth from one of those.

I search my pockets for change, then I step up. I pick at random: Hot Fries, why not? My stomach grumbles, but between the both of us, it knows I'm going to eat a banana instead. The Hot Fries will go to Arden or in the trash. It just feels good to do something normal. Take a road trip, buy some snacks at a rest stop. All around me, people are doing the same thing.

Families buzz, and a couple girls my age walk a dog up and down the grass. Their clothes are neon-bright, their hair pulled into intricate hairdos. They have spirit paint on their face— they're a team or a group or something. Maybe they're heading to cheerleading camp. Or an archery competition. A dance battle. Whatever, it's one more stop on the way to the rest of their lives.

Walking past them, I wave and I say, "Pretty dog."

"Thanks," one replies. She smiles, her teeth white and straight.

For just a second, I wish I could follow her. Maybe go to their jamboree, too. Two steps behind, I could trail her forever—to Homecoming in the fall, and to check the mail with her until she gets the acceptance letter from her second-choice college. She gets waitlisted at her first choice, and she cries. It's not the end of the world, though. She takes second place, and that's awesome because she gets there and her roommate is strange and cool, and being free is strange and cool, and . . .

Then I have to stop, because I can't wrap my head around college. What happens there. That's the end of Girl with Dog's story, from my perspective, anyway. The split second is over, and I'm back in my own life.

And I have no idea how my story ends anymore. The nice, clean break of cancer bailed on me. Now I can do anything, anywhere, except I don't know anything, or anyone. An unbearable well of sadness threatens to rise up. Sometimes, I get mad. I feel like, if I could just punch hard enough, things would get better. Then I laugh at myself for my own stupidity.

Hiking toward the parking lot, I see Arden leaning against the car. She's still wearing her headband, but some of her curls have escaped. They dance and dance; her shoulders roll subtly. She's texting somebody at warp speed. My despair retreats, because no, I have no fucking clue what happens next. But unlike last week, I know how I'm getting there.

Right now, it's in a Honda Civic. It's along the last piece of the Eisenhower Interstate System, over the river, through the woods. And it's with someone. That girl right there, with the soft smile and strong jaw, and long fingers with nubbly knuckles.

The breath goes out of me because I realize, I wanna kiss that smile. And touch her hair. I wanna lay in the dark with her, and share our breath and our secrets. I want secrets with her; I want *her*.

I'm falling in love with Arden Trochessett. And I'm done worrying about why.

"Say hey," I call to her.

When Arden raises her head, she lights with a smile. I'm not going to waste time telling you again how pretty she is—I've already done that; it's still true. This time, I'll tell you that I *feel* it, though. Her smile slips right through my breastbone. My heart fibrillates, which is a shitty word for the sensation, but an accurate one. It's on high pulse, faster than racing. I wonder what it feels like to her, when she looks at me. Does it feel like anything at all?

"Hey!" She holds up her phone. "Guess what I just did."

"Nope. Just tell me."

When I come closer, she leans in and turns the screen to me. There's a big black SUV splashed across it. It looks like an urban destroyer, a tank to battle the wilds of Whole Foods and muddy soccer fields. Catching my eye, Arden smiles. "We're picking that up in St. Louis."

My mouth drops open. "No way."

Pleased, Arden nods and flips through a few more pictures. "I'm serious. We're going to deliver it to Grand Junction, Colorado. They're going to reimburse us for gas *and* pay us five hundred bucks to get it there before Saturday."

This sounds way too good to be true. It's like those signs that say *Free Fish Fry*, only you get there and have to listen to a sermon first. Yeah, you'll get the fish, but it's not really free. Shoving my hands in my back pockets, I look at the phone's screen again. "Are you sure this is legit?"

"Positive." Arden pushes off the car, just about beaming. "It was a job listing in my dad's database. I snagged it before he saw it."

"Database? What exactly does your dad do for a living?"

"He mostly goes to meetings. But the company he owns is a custom courier service. If you have something precious and you want it to get somewhere, anywhere, all over the world, personally hand-delivered by a human being, you call Trochessett & Tyler. Like, last year, he drove a crate full of Rembrandts from New York to Boston."

"Too bad they weren't *van Goghs*," I joke, but it's lame and Arden doesn't laugh. "Because the van goes . . . forget it."

"Anyway," Arden says, opening her door, "I told the guy we'd give him a fifty-percent discount if he paid us in cash. You want to know what's funny?"

Sliding into the passenger seat again, I toss the Hot Fries in her direction. "That some crackhead is willing to pay a thousand bucks so somebody else can drive his car?"

"People pay more than that, but no. What's funny is that I told him half up front, half when we deliver the car. I learned that from you."

Now it's my turn to be proud. I hold up a hand for a high five. When I get it, I tangle my fingers in hers. A big spark jolts through me when she doesn't pull away. In fact, she manages to get in, get buckled, and get the car started, and she doesn't once let go.

I change my mind. We're pulling back on the highway and I change my mind—I'm not falling for Arden.

I think I already fell.

# (2038.67)

**We're almost there, almost to Vandalia. Every time we** pass a new mileage sign, I twitch. Even though I'm just gonna give her directions to something, I feel like I'm giving her a present. It's what I have; I can't buy her anything she can't buy herself. But I can give her a quest; I can give her this.

It's getting dark, and I blow bubbles from the passenger's seat. The koosh ball I lost in the back, but the bubbles were lying right on top of the bag, begging me to play. The cap resting on the dashboard, the bottle tucked between my knees, I dip the wand into soapy water while I ask her twenty questions. Dip; exhale. Silvery globes stream toward her, the little ones catching in her hair.

"Cheeseburger or pizza?" I ask.

Brushing away bubbles, she furrows her brows. "Like, right now, or that's the only thing I get forever?"

Dip. "Both." Blow.

Our Honda started shaking a couple miles back. It's not bad yet. Just a vibration, mostly noticeable when I glance in the rearview mirror. Everything in it is fuzzy, like I'm looking through the bottom of a Coke bottle. The questions keep both our minds off the shimmy. *Little Honda Civic*, I pray, *keep it together, all right?*

Finally, Arden says, "Neither."

I yelp in disbelief, and lose the bubble wand in the bottle. Sloshing my finger around after it, I boggle at her. "Why neither?"

"Because," Arden says with a shrug. "If I want greasy meat and cheese, I want to be able to choose. If I had to have a cheeseburger when I wanted pizza, I'd hate that."

"So you're just picking none."

"Better to have loved and lost," she teases.

She's out of her mind and I love it. I start to dip the wand again when I see the sign I've been waiting for. Grabbing her arm, I slosh bubble water all down my hand but that's fine! It'll wash off. "Take this exit! Take it!"

Arden veers as I scramble to put the lid back on. My eyes are wide open, my heart beats fast, We made it to Vandalia, Illinois, and that means we're going to see a dragon.

Let me explain something, because it's important. Since the beginning, it's been me and Arden and dragons. Seems to me like the first time we talked was in Barrens chat. The Barrens is . . . well, it *was* . . . one step up from newbie village. Fantasyland middle school. When everybody gets to typing in the public chat, you can tell why twelve-year-old boys ain't making foreign policy, is all I'm saying.

The only reason I noticed Arden in the scroll was, she was looking for somebody to try to sneak into Onyxia's Lair. Big-ass, bad-ass, black-ass dragon. It took forty people to kill Onyxia back then. The elite guilds that did it would truck out there, then come back to the cities to hang up the dragon's head to celebrate. And Arden, who was level 14 instead of 60, and a party of one instead of forty, was trying to get people to go take a look with her.

She kept asking and asking, and finally I sent her a private message. "I'll go."

In reply, she invited me to her group. Nobody else wanted to go—because they weren't stupid, mostly. The fact was, it was guaranteed death. We were lowbies, and we had to walk all the way to Dustwallow Marsh because we didn't have mounts yet. And then we got killed ninety-seven times in a row, because guess what? A level-60 dungeon raid usually sits in the middle of a zone full of level-60 monsters.

We never even made it to the cave. But we had a hell of a time on the trip, so I added her to my friends list. Every time her name popped up, I had to message her. Just because she impressed me; we were crazy, both of us, and it was cool to finally be crazy with company. Pretty soon, we were logging on at the same time, on purpose.

Since then, we've managed to see Onyxia (and get our asses kicked), and we saw Nefarian (and got our asses kicked). We camped in Ferelas forever, until Arden got her green baby dragonkin pet. Then we spent a shit-ton of time grinding rep on the Timeless Isle so we could fly around on giant Chinese dragons.

So, yeah. Dragons. It's a *thing*.

And because of that, we're driving into small-town Illinois, to see the Kaskaskia Dragon. I wanna grab Arden's hand, because the tension's killing me, no kidding. But she has to make a sharp turn, and I have to worry, kicking the Skittles and making them rattle like my bottle of pills. That sound, it's a rattlesnake warning—*don't get your hopes up. Don't get excited.*

For once, that warning is wrong. We cut out on the main drag, and shit, it's epic. This vast green field stretches out, and there it is. Spines, a tail, a head with glittering chrome teeth. Outlined by streetlights in the dark, this beast, this *thing*, it's made out of sheet metal and polished mirror bright. The head raises up into the air, the tail curls to a point.

It's a dragon. It's a *dragon*.

Arden parks and we pile out of the car, nearly stumbling over each other. We have to get closer, look at it, touch it. As we're crossing the green grass to get there, a rumble fills the air. Sounds like a hot-water heater lighting up. There's a *ting-ting-ting*, and then a gorge of fire spews from the dragon's mouth. It billows out, curling and twisting, real fire up there in the air. A few seconds later, it stops abruptly.

"Are. You. Serious?" Arden whispers.

A moment. Total silence.

And then I laugh. I laugh and laugh, because fuck me. It's a fire-breathing dragon. Standing right there, in the middle of a field in Illinois, it's a *fire-breathing dragon*. When we get closer, we discover there's a slot in it. It takes *dragon tokens* to light it up. We end up racing each other to a nearby liquor store to buy some. Underage? Who cares; we're not here for the whiskey. We're here for the fairy gold.

Arden drops ten bucks for ten tokens and we bolt for the field again. I can't remember the last time I ran, not for real. Not on my actual legs, and I'm sweating like crazy. But it's good. It's good, because Arden's laughing, and I'm standing back with her phone and we try to time it. Drop the token, wait for the fire, *hurry up get the picture.*

The first couple suck. I just stand in my pictures, because I'm already out of breath. Arden, though, she gets the timing down. On her third go, she waits for the fire then tips up on her hands. Toes pointed straight in the air, body cutting the sky like a knife, she holds the position until the flames die. She bounces to her feet and digs in her pocket for another coin.

Her face is so flushed, and she feeds the dragon again. This time, she does the handstand on *one* freaking hand, and I barely get the picture taken because I'm so busy gaping. The next picture, I fail straight out. One second, Arden's on both her feet, and the next, she's flipping over backwards. To hell with gravity. The dragon made her strong. She can fly now.

A guy with a wispy beard steps up next to me. "You guys want a picture together?"

I hesitate. He said guys, but maybe he woulda said that no matter what? And giving somebody your phone is a good way to let somebody steal your phone. Thanks to me, Arden already lost a car. She loses her iPhone, and there's probably gonna be some words.

There are, just not the ones I expect.

"Do it, Dylan!" Arden waves me over. "Come on!"

Reluctantly, I hand off the phone and take two slow steps, waiting for Wispy to bolt. Instead, he holds up the phone and waits for me to get into position. I jog to Arden's side and try to figure out where to stand. Before I know it, she drapes her arm over my shoulder and hauls me in closer.

"Where did you learn to do all that?" I whisper.

With a squeeze, she says, "Summer camp."

"What *didn't* you do at summer camp, boo?"

Arden laughs. She smells good and feels warm, and there's so much glow around her right now. I bathe in it. In goes the token, here comes the fire.

"Smile," Wispy says, and honestly, I'd like to see him stop me.

# (THE DIFFERENCE BETWEEN ANTICIPATION AND DREAD.)

**This has been the longest day in the damned universe,** but the signs say we're almost to Missouri, and I'm buzzing. The car is too, shaking even more now when Arden gets it over 65. I think it knows we're about to abandon it. I'm gonna be so pissed if it breaks down while we're still in Illinois. I asked it for *one* thing, all right? One! It only needs to make it to St. Louis, so I can see the Arch.

"I've been waiting for this the whole trip," I tell Arden, straining against the seat belt to watch the horizon.

"So much for our dragon," she says, playing mournful.

"Don't be like that. I'm just saying, this is—" I stop. How do I even explain it? There's stuff like the dragon, fucking *amazing*, but out of place. Or out of time; it's something imagination made happen, and if you get too far away, it just doesn't exist anymore. Go ahead, ask somebody if they ever heard of the Kaskaskia Dragon. "It's forever, you know? It was here before we were born and it's gonna be here way after we die."

"This is seriously your first monument?" Of course, she has the right word for it. "Haven't you seen the Statue of Liberty?"

"No." I tear myself away from the window to look at her. "I'm not kidding. I haven't ever been *anywhere*. I never saw an ocean, or the Empire State Building, or Mount Rushmore . . ."

"Which is in the Dakotas," she says with a smirk. "Which we're skipping, bee tee dubs. I hear there's nothing there."

"Don't be a smart-ass," I say.

"Better than a dumb-ass," she crows. Arden takes both hands off the wheel to stretch. We've been going awhile now. She's starting to fade, and that's all right. That means a night in St. Louis. Even though we're gonna find a hotel and crash, it still sounds amazing. The quest says we have to stop for a night and pay tribute to the great Arch.

The traffic builds up around us. I noticed that happening around Cincinnati and Indianapolis, too. You can go miles and miles with just a couple other cars around you. As soon as you roll up on a city, cars come out of nowhere. They fill up the lanes, and trap you behind slow-ass chicken trucks and old ladies in massive Cadillacs.

Arden's phone rings, and she picks it up. Her posture stays the same, but a frown slips into her voice. "No, man, what's up?" Mouthing to me, I think she says that *it's my friend Jagger*. I could be wrong, though. I never learned to read lips, and I get distracted looking at Arden's.

There are good-looking guys in my neighborhood, sort of. I grew up with them. They're kinda rough. Some of 'em smell like Marlboro Lights. But I remember them with fat baby faces and missing teeth. I know who crapped their pants the first day of school. Who still calls the place with all the books a li*berry*. They work on their cars in the street, and set off Fourth of July fireworks starting June fifteenth or so. I'm not any better than them, and they probably see a horror show when they look at me.

But Arden's here, outside the game, and she brought the magic with her. There are real dragons; I'm gonna touch this arch, and me and her, we're gonna spend another night together. We're gonna share a bed again; I feel like I'm not taking anything for granted, thinking that. We'll touch; her breath will skim my cheek. Maybe I'll steal her headband and wrap it around one wrist, because it smells good—because it smells like her.

I swim my dreamy brain back up to the surface and just eavesdrop. Right now, Arden's thanking (possibly) Jagger for covering for her. The conversation is hard to follow with only half of it. I think he played it off when he ran into Arden's dad somewhere, like he knew all about Dylan and the lake house.

Interestingly, Arden lowers her voice and glances at me and says, "Yeah, he's hot."

"We're hooking up now? Fuck yeah," I say with a grin, but not too loud.

I rest my head against the window and peer at myself in the side mirror. Mostly, I'm making sure I still look like I was put together in the dark. Big shock, I do.

Sometimes, I think that should bother me more. There's a dead space in my heart where that's supposed to go, I guess. By the time I was old enough to give a shit how I looked, I was glad to just be alive. Now that I'm gonna stay alive, the emptiness is just what *could* have been.

Maybe in another life, where I didn't get sick, I grew up good to look at. I grew up and got cut, but not too much. Enough, just enough so guys looked my way. In this life, though, I never was cute, and I never hooked up at school, and the only guy I ever kissed is dead. It just is.

I like the way Arden tells it. In her version of my life, I'm something to want. Something to brag about.

"You haven't met him, and you're not going to," she says, puffed up and possessive. "Why? Because you're a slag, and I don't trust you alone with him."

She says all of this with a lying smile, with laughter threaded in her voice. Part of me wonders if she means any of this; part of me desperately wants it to be true. It's not. It can't be, I don't think. Logic says though, if she's saying it in front of me, it's because it's easy to say—it's not how she really feels. She might hold all her friends' hands. As soon as that thought rises up, jealousy starts to burn in my belly. She has other *friends*.

*That* makes me jealous. Or, envious? People say there's a difference, but like lay and lie and affect and effect, damned if I can keep it straight. Let's put it this way: you know what I mean, so leave it alone. Short version is, I don't get to keep Arden to myself. She's not all mine.

Hanging up, Arden tosses the phone into the console again. The smile falls off her face and she turns to me. Venomous and tense, she says, "God, I hate him."

"Seriously? You sounded like besties."

"I just get stuck hanging with him."

Flattening her lips, Arden shifts lanes abruptly, speeding around a car that's toodling along too slow. Around us, the flatness suddenly drops away. Hills appear from nothing, signaling a change of geography. We're elevated now, passing over trees and train tracks alike. I'm not jealous anymore, but I'm confused. And I ache, because it's obvious Arden's hurting. I just don't know what to say. Maybe I don't have anything to say, so I talk shit. That, I can do.

"I get stuck sitting with my mother's best friend's niece sometimes," I tell her. Lynne doesn't bring Lolly around much. Just when her sister decides to ride long-distance with her trucker boyfriend. As much as I loathe Lynne, Lolly is actually okay. She has carroty red hair, and she draws her eyeliner on the waterline. That's all I have to say about her. We have nothing to talk about. She doesn't game, I don't watch reality shows. Neither of us wants to make out with the other.

"Dylan?" She catches her lower lip in her teeth. She bites down so hard, the blood drains away, and then she lets it spring free. "I might not go back."

The *way* she says it worries me. It sounds *final.* Too final. My insides turn, anxious and tightening by the moment. Licking my dry lips, I say, "You wouldn't be the first person to run away to California."

Arden nods and leans her head back against the rest. Guiding the wheel with her fingertips, she becomes a statue. Still flesh, eyes unblinking. Whatever's happening in her head, she doesn't share.

I am the last person in the world to save somebody. But that look scares me. I reach out anyway, brave or stupid, and brush the back of my hand against her rough cheek.

"You okay?"

She says nothing. Then, with her eyes still on the road, she turns her head slightly, her lips rasping against my hand. "I'm fine. Swear."

I want to believe her. I want to so bad.

# (1968.51)

**At Arden's insistence, we park for the Arch. I saw it** from a distance first, a silvery loop on the other side of the Mississippi.

Turns out, it has its own name: the Gateway Arch. Gateway to the West, see thirty miles all around and 200 years into the past. It's not as old as I thought it was; it was built in the 1960s. I don't know why, but I thought it had been here a hundred years. Maybe more. Doesn't matter, though, because it's still epic.

Standing beneath it, I tip my head all the way back. So far back, I lose my balance. With a few uneasy steps, I steady myself and drink it in. Polished steel shimmers, floodlights caressing it all the way up. It's taller than I imagined. Seeing pictures didn't tell the truth; yeah, in pictures, the people are tiny and the *monument* is big. But this is legendary. It's enormous; so big, you can go inside and ride up to the top.

"People built that," I say to Arden. I shake my head to soothe my neck, then look up again. I can't get enough of it. It's a wonder of my world. Imaginary until now, and now the most amazing thing I've ever seen.

Arden puts a hand on the small of my back when I stumble again. Her touch spreads warmth through my t-shirt, a gentle brand on my skin. "I know, right? I wouldn't have wanted to be the guy putting the last piece on, would you?"

Confidently, I tell her, "I'm not afraid of heights."

"I'm not either," she says with a thoughtful smile. "I'm more afraid I'll jump."

What a strange, exhilarating confession. Sometimes in the game, I feel that way. Like a tall place is just waiting for me to leap from it. Drowning in the game scares me, but jumping off of stuff just lights me up. But that's in the game. We fall down; we die, we run back and start again. This is real life, and this shit is real tall.

"Even that high?" I ask her.

"Especially that high."

Looking away from the gleam of the Arch, I reach back and rub Arden's hand. "Seriously? You'd stand up there and have to convince yourself not to jump. Like, 'No, me! Don't jump.'"

Arden laughs incredulously. "Exactly! I'll jump off anything." She points out a curb. "Like that. Or a balcony. Or a cliff. I don't know what it is. I just stand on the edge, look down and it's in my head. *Jump. Do it. Go for it.*"

"Just don't forget that you'll pop like a watermelon if you do," I say. "You're prettier when you're not inside out."

"Go out with me," she says. The intensity surprises me, how it hardens her all over. A deep breath spreads her shoulders wide and her eyes darken. They do; they're alive with shadows and flashes of color that dazzle me. She's a kaleidoscope; she changes everything.

Now I'm afraid. It could be a joke. I could be misunderstanding. (Let's face it, I could be hallucinating. My forehead still hurts from running into my ghost-that-wasn't when I was looking for the pool.) I feel fragile and hollow and too full, all at the same time.

Scrubbing my hands against my hips, I squint at her. "I *am* out with you."

"Don't play dumb, Dylan," she grumbles. Then, in case that was the wrong thing to say (it kind of was), she softens it. "I mean, let's go to a movie. Let's have dinner. Let's hold hands."

There's no pause in Azeroth, and there's no pause here, either. But I'm frozen—with fear. With hope. Everything I've been feeling for her, it's been easy to say it's just mine. One-sided, because why wouldn't it be? Look at her. Fucking look at her, really, and listen to her laugh and follow the train of her thoughts, and try not to fall in love. But look at me and . . . what the hell is she seeing when she looks at *me?*

Then all at once, I melt. I don't know why Arden wants to take me to the movies (maybe she's been in my drugs?), but I don't care. I've been dying for years. In a real and present sense, not in a country song, *live like it might be your last, nobody knows the day and time* way.

I'm here now. I'll be here next month; I'll be here next year. Arden is beautiful and confusing and I want her to be mine.

There's time. I have *time* to figure it out. Judge me if you want to (if you haven't already, let's be fair, you have a lot you could hold against me at this point), but I step into Arden's space. She's taller than I am.

Reaching out, I lace our hands together. I rest my temple against hers and shiver when her hair brushes my skin. I can't help myself. She's so clean, so warm, and I say, "Tonight?"

# (TONIGHT)

**We grab our stuff and say good-bye to the Civic. It was a** good-bad car, and now it'll be somebody else's. We leave the doors unlocked and the keys inside, in case somebody wants to go on a joyride. In case somebody else is running from California to Maryland, and they need a set of wheels to get them through Indiana and Pennsylvania.

Arden calls a cab and we check into a hotel first. Not the way most dates go, but who wants to cart a cooler and a backpack and a laptop all over town? Not us, let me tell you. It's another medium-okay hotel, no cookies in the foyer, though.

Even when I don't want to eat them, it's nice to smell them. So points off for no cookies.

I shower after Arden does. The steam smells like her, and it makes me jittery. All over, I'm warm, and it's not just the water spilling over my bare skin. It's like I can feel her, arms banding around me, heart beating beneath my ear. My breath is short and I bite my lip again and again. By the time I get out and towel off, I'm wound tight.

When I walk out that bathroom door, I don't know what to expect. I've spent most of my nights with Arden for the last couple years. Maybe I crushed on her before, but the game puts a weird shine on that. We've done nothing but flirt for years, in completely different bodies. In cities where warlocks are raining fire down for fun, and people fly by on magic carpets.

For me, Arden was purple-haired and decayed, but I smiled when I saw her anyway. When I logged in, I knew she'd be waiting for me. Or I'd wait for her, and then we'd dive into this vast, enchanted world.

Limited by programmed emotions and actions, we only fit together in predestined ways. She could tell me /jokes, and I could blow her a /kiss. Even if I had wanted to hold her hand before, I couldn't. All we could do was sit close together and type in message.

But that's *Arden* out there—the same, but different. I steel myself and step into the room. Even though we're not getting fancy or dressing up or anything, we know we're coming back to the hotel together, I'm nervous. She looks nervous too, her smile rising and falling as she struggles to come up with something to say.

Instead of letting her wild hair fly free, she's tied it back. She looks older that way, not as soft. But now her face is bared; I see all of her features, no shadows at all. My insides dip again, and for the first time, I wish, I wish so hard, that she could look at me and feel the same way. If she can look past all my bones and edges, then good for her. But I wish she was getting the full blast of crazy beautiful that I am. It might even things up a bit.

Neither of us speaks. That unsteady, anxious quiet from our very first day in the flesh is back. It's only a few steps from me to her, but we don't try to make it. Instead, we look each other over. As if we're going to see something new or different, but what? It's the same clothes we bought at Walmart, and we're the same selves we've been since I turned up on her doorstep.

"So," Arden says.

"Yeah . . . ," I reply.

I'm selfish. I want this to be amazing, and right now, it's just awkward. So I make myself say something. Somebody has to,

248

may as well be me. Since we started in Warcraft, and it makes sense to us, I crib from that.

"You have beautiful skin," I tell her, one of the Undead pickup lines from the game turned back on her. "No maggot holes at all."

The tension burns away. She breaks into a smile. Instead of heading for the door without me, she holds out her hand. She meant it, every word she said, she meant it. Until I take that hand, she's going to wait for me. She smiles; she teases, "I barely recognize you without your horns."

Slipping my fingers into hers, I swell from the inside when she tightens her grip in mine. This is a thing that's happening. She wasn't messing around; we're going out. To dinner, to a movie, just the two of us. I'm dizzy all the way down the elevator, and when we climb into yet another cab, I think twice, but fuck it. I go ahead and pull her beneath my arm.

While we showered, dark slipped over St. Louis. The city lights wash it clean; the sky is clear and studded with stars. It's a different world than we drove into, transformed after sunset just like Azeroth. Arden curled to my side and both of us watching the world pass us through the cab's windows, I smile.

At night, the river is silver.

# ( . . . )

**She forgives me when I sleep through the movie. I for-**give her when she orders sushi.

# (LEAP)

**Everything we talk about is stupid and inconsequential.**
You don't believe me, so I'll prove it. In the cab back to the
hotel, I'm drunk and dying over the way she works her fingers
between mine. Her fingertips are so soft, skimming through
my palm, and then looping back to graze my wrist.

What matters is that when I reach for her, she reaches back. Our
hands slip together. Then apart, trailing and tracing. Racing to
find new ways to meet between us. When it's quiet, it's audible. Skin whispering on skin, rasped together, slipped apart.
Seeking again in a tumble of electric sensation. Sometimes I get
brave, and skim up the inside of her arm—never too far, not
too far. Touching the inside of her elbow is impossibly thrilling.

And at the same time, I say, "I kinda like knowing who the King of England is gonna be in sixty years."

Angled toward me, Arden presses her thumb against my wrist. Looking up through her dark brows, she murmurs, "I had no idea you cared about the royal family."

We inch closer, until we're resting our brows against each other's. We can't look anywhere but into our eyes, now. It's a raw and naked sensation, better than adrenaline. Better than oxies. Better than getting better. Being short of breath right now is a good thing. It means something is going right for once.

With a crooked smile, I shrug and press back against her thumb. "I don't really. It's just like—I can see the future, you know? I know King George is gonna be there. If I know it, then I'm part of it. I'll still be here."

"You will be here," she says. Her gaze falls, even as she turns her hand in mine. "You got better."

"That's still a long time from now. Who knows if I'll—"

She shushes me. "If somebody remembers your name, you live forever."

"Who's going to—" I start.

She interrupts, placing her finger on my lips. There are so many shades of green in her eyes. Spring and summer, jungle and countryside. She's all brown and green, her hair, her eyes—her skin smooth; she's alive. With a tender touch, she unfolds my hand and presses it against her collarbone. Her lashes dip, hiding her eyes, then revealing them again. They're a wonder every time. "I will."

A whisper slips out of me; I'm surprised. I don't mean to say it this way, it just happens. Like it was sitting, coiled in the dark frame of my body, waiting to spring out. Dylan-in-the-box, unstoppable, uncontrollable. "I'm afraid."

It's the least romantic thing I can say. Even swept up in her, it's there. I can't stop picking at it, even when I'm one breath away from a kiss. If I just shut up and leaned in, it would happen. Aching and wanting and needing, it feels like bad luck to just be here with her and stop thinking.

It's just, I know if I kiss her now then I'm not trembling on the edge, wanting it. Her kiss is something to anticipate. To look forward to.

No, not to live for, because that's putting way too much pressure on it. This isn't the fairy-tale cut, where I die and she cries and love revives me. No, this is just regular old selfish *enjoying the want*. And how much it hurts to want it, especially after I tried not to. Especially because it's terrifying and beautiful and maddening to know it *will* happen but not knowing exactly when.

Drawing our joined hands up between us, she rests her chin against them. Now her breath trails heat along my fingers, a new experience, just as good. "Me too. All the time."

She has everything that seems important, so what's scary about being beautiful Arden Trochessett? The answer is being *Arden* Trochessett. Not David. Not Nuba. It's been there all along. It dances on the edge of her expressions. She shuts herself down so fast, I only catch glimpses of it. When she lets it get out, it scares me. If she stood at the edge of a cliff, she'd jump.

*I hope, I hope, I hope . . .*

I hope I'm not the cliff she's standing on.

# (BUT THAT THOUGHT
ISN'T OVER)

**Well, if I am, I'll quake. I'll roll her off the edge. I'll grow** and grow, till I touch the sky, till she can't climb anymore. There's a right way and a wrong way to protect her, and I think I'm starting to get the difference now. Swallowing hard, I ask— and I really want to know—"What scares you?"

"I'm afraid to want things. If I need something, I sit there quietly, needing it. If I'm lucky, somebody notices."

"Why?" I trail my free hand up, twining it around Arden's wrist. She's caught in my touch, bound to me. "I don't—I walked into your house, and I was like, you have everything. Every single thing in the world, you know?"

Furrowing her brow, she says, "Nobody loves *me*. I don't mean, awww, poor Arden, poor little rich girl. I mean *me*. I thought I had my Mom, but she walked away. And she did it like it was so easy. Dad sticks around because he has to. You met him. You know what he's like.

"All the friends I had before the divorce, they're gone. The friends I have now . . . I hate them. And that makes me a terrible person, but it's like, we're only friends because we're the only ones in school. I would never tell Jagger anything that mattered to me, because he'd use it against me. He's just . . . that's who he is."

When Arden smiles this time, it's weighted. Weary. Her eyes shine, but this time because there's tears in them. "So if I'm quiet enough and I don't ask for anything, maybe I can just be a ghost. I can be inside myself, and be near people, even if they don't know I'm there, and I can still be *me* because I don't make a sound."

I know what it's like to have nobody left. What I don't understand is why the rest of the world isn't falling for Arden. I work my hand free and fan my fingers across her cheek. My thumb skims the corner of her lips and I tell her, "*I* love you."

"Dylan—" she protests, but I cut her off.

"Shut up. I'm not talking about goo-goo kissy-face, I'm saying, you're my friend. You're my *best* friend. All my most important memories are with you. I lay around all day waiting for you to get home from school or piano practice or whatever. When you log into the game, my day starts.

"And now . . . when you wake up next to me, my day starts. And if you went along with this because you were afraid to tell me no, you should say it right now, okay? We'll go back. We'll go back right fucking now. Even if everybody else in your life disappoints you, I don't want to. I won't."

"You don't," she says, and she sounds so broken. Her eyes shine, and I guess I'm not the only one who cries over shit that can't be fixed.

Shifting, I sling an arm around her neck and pull her in. I tuck her head beneath my chin and do my best to hold her. The backseat of a cab isn't the most elegant place to do this, but oh well. This is where we are. Soaking her up, I tighten my arms around her like I can keep the rest of the world away.

"It's okay," I lie, but I mean it.

Her breath is humid on my throat, and her hair slips, silky against my cheek. When her shoulders shake, I quiver; I rub her back and will away the dark for her. I can't actually do it; she knows it, but so what?

Sometimes all that matters is that somebody wants to try.

# (B A N A N A S)

**I don't kiss her and she doesn't kiss me. We sleep in a** tight, tangled knot and when she wakes up, she's full of fire. I'm not sure what she's doing on the computer, but she's typing like a demon is whipping her. Me? I'm exhausted. Slept all night, and wore myself out sleeping, nice. I roll out of bed and wolf down a banana that fuck me, *tastes like a banana.* An actual goddamned banana.

It's like the lights turned on. Like somebody's lighting a fire in the boiler, and opening up the windows and letting the air in for the first time in years. That's the best banana I've had since elementary school and it almost makes me weep. I want another banana. I want to eat stuff and hang out and *be here.* I want to keep my promises. I want to be the one who stays.

With a quick look at Arden— she's all buried deep in the internet— I rise to my feet. Arden barely glances over before looking back to the screen. That's when I pull my meds out of the backpack. I measure my steps, because I don't want Arden to hear the pills rattle in the bottle. And that bottle is heavy. It's been an anchor for a long time now, dragging out after me.

I creep into the bathroom and turn on the water. There I am in the mirror, angled out, clutching prescriptions like they're holy. Inside, my bones and my blood protest. My head aches, just a little. Like a threat. There's all kinds of reasons to keep these on hand. Didn't I snap at Arden about it? I should keep them because they're mine. Because they're valuable. And some not-very-secret part of me has been thinking—because being better might be a lie.

Spontaneous remission probably doesn't happen overnight, but it seems like it. One appointment, all the X-rays and MRIs look like Christmas trees, lit up with tumors and mets. But you're stable, nothing's getting worse so they send you home to keep dying in slow motion. Come back a month later, two months later, and somebody took the lights down.

Everybody talks low, and hushed—but nobody calls the Pope, because this happens. Not a lot. But enough that they have a name for it; enough that they make the next appointment six months out. (Last time, you didn't have six months left.) So they write your last script for pills, and the nurse gives you a sheet so you can detox, and you're on your own.

I'm on my own. And all this time, I've been waiting to need these drugs again.

"I got better," I tell the mirror. Better, better, better, I twist open the cap and stand there— daring myself to jump. Pouring tablets into my hand, I consider popping one or two for the road. Just for old time's sake, but no. I'm done; I'm done dying, I'm done being sick. I'm done with sleeping and giving up everything to a body that tried to kill me, no. I'm in charge now.

I dump my pills in the toilet.

Panic fills my chest and I hurry to flush. It takes four, five flushes to get them to all go down. The whole time, I'm convincing myself not to reach into the pot, not to grab a couple out, just in case JUST IN CASE. But I don't. I don't, because I don't need it anymore. Never again; I got *better*.

Somewhere, Lynne is screaming in agony and she doesn't know why. That's a thought that makes me feel good. Try to sell them now, Lynne. Good luck with that.

I dump the empty bottle beneath the sink. After that, I wash my hands real slow, and then my face. Then I stare at myself for a minute again. I look exactly the same. Exactly the same as I did before, but fuck it. I feel lighter. I feel alive. I feel like another banana, actually.

We're gonna have to get more, because I don't stop at two.

# (OUTLINES)

**"I've been thinking," Arden says.**

She slides into bed next to me. After my big adventure in the bathroom, I plowed back into the sheets to curl up. I wasn't tired, but I had to keep my nervous, anxious energy in check somehow. I devoured all the bananas; I almost started on the last of the oranges, and thought better of it. Here we are in a hotel room; here we are with this nice bed—*Maybe, I thought, Arden will lay with me. Maybe her lips will brush against the back of my neck.*

Instead, she sits, her elbow stitching against my side. "How are we going to find this ship?"

I sway to the rhythms of her fingers on a keyboard. It's a good question. A real good question; I moan and roll against her. Now her elbow mostly rests on top of my head. "I don't know. It didn't say in the quest text. I thought we'd just wander in the desert until we found it."

"We're going to find it the same way you picked this route," she informs me. There's a hint of pride in her voice as she continues. "Online satellite maps; I read a story on Cracked a while back. Archaeologists are finding lost cities and stuff by looking at satellite maps. They can see the outlines, even if the stuff is buried, right?"

"How do you spell that? Archaeologist?" I ask. I briefly wonder what would happen if I bit her. Not hard; I don't want to hurt her. I just kinda wanna bite her a little bit. It's a crazy, stupid thought, one that comes out of nowhere, and goes right back into the shadows. Maybe later, I'll ask Arden if she wonders terrible things. That's a topic all by itself.

Amused, she looks at me. "Are we spelling, or are you checking out how smart I am?"

"You're really, really smart," I tell her. I want to bury my face against her waist and fall asleep again. The shivery thrill that runs through me only has a little to do with being pressed this close to Arden. Instead, I push the pillow away and blink up at her. "Show me."

Angling the laptop so I can see it, she jabs a finger at a darkish spot in the middle of beige. Lots and lots of beige. It takes me a minute to focus and realize what I'm looking at. It's the desert, around the Salton Sea. Where the Colorado River used to flood into it and doesn't anymore. There are lots of random shapes in the image. But Arden's finger rests on top of one that looks like half a teardrop.

"That," she says, "That could be a ship."

Slowly, I push myself to sitting. With shaky hands, I take the laptop and lean in to look again. Harder. Closer. Holy shit.

It could be. Why couldn't it be? Lots of people have gone looking for this thing. Some people claim they found it and lost it again. Why can't it be *that* shape in the desert, right there on an internet map? When my heart starts to pound, I feel it in my throat. "Holy shit, Arden. Holy shit."

Excited, she tips the screen. "I know, right?"

"We gotta go," I tell her. I'm all kinds of beauty and grace when I'm in a hurry. When I throw the blankets aside, they don't get all the way aside. They tangle around my legs twined like ivy. Instead of landing on my feet and standing up, I hit the floor. It would be nice if the floor turned into quicksand and just sucked me down; I'd love to disappear into it and pretend I didn't just take a header.

Arden yelps. The bed bounces and all of a sudden she's over me. Hands under my arms, she struggles to lift me up. Now it's twice as embarrassing, because I think she thinks there's something wrong. She's not half-laughing, like you do when you're startled. She's serious, all business, strong hands freeing me from the scourge of the bedspread and trying to set me right. "Are you all right?"

Other than being humiliated, I'm great. I roll my eyes at myself, and try to get her to smile. "I'm fine. I just wanted to see if you'd feel me up."

She doesn't laugh. Instead, she asks, "Are you sure?"

Maybe I'm not funny. I kinda always thought I was. Fingers tangling in her hair, I nod. "I'm good. I'm clumsy; that's all."

My sweat smells sharp; I'm still wrinkled from sleep. My morning-banana breath has got to be epic. And in spite of all that, Arden pulls me close and leans down to kiss me. The glimmer of electric fire washes over my lips, and I want it. I want this kiss, right now, because either she's the most desperate motherfucker in the universe or she really likes me.

But I nudge my forehead against hers and ward it off. Last night wasn't right; this isn't either. I know there's a moment out there. It's suspended, flickering like a star just at the horizon. That kiss doesn't taste like worry or concern; it's just honey. It's pure. But I don't want Arden to think I don't want it, because I do. More than anything. I murmur to her, "Not yet, okay?"

When she breathes, her body presses against mine. Her fingers press into my bony shoulders. "Not no?"

"Not no," I say.

So I don't kiss her, and she doesn't kiss me. Not yet.

# (ROAD CONVERSATIONS)

**Stupid, morbid things are funny sometimes. Out of** nowhere, Arden asks, "Did you ever watch that show, *Dead Like Me*?"

It's out of her mouth before she realizes what she said. Oh shit, oh no. She mentioned the D-word. Mortality is real out here, oh hell no—it's one thing to do it in the game, but not now. She telegraphs worry; no, she waves those flags. Her face is bright and open with it.

In the split second before she takes it back, I say, "Nah. Too busy watching *The Walking Dead*."

Arden catches on quick. This is a game we've played before:

link up the words, run with it as far as you can take it. One night, we had an epic thread of *baby* that started with titles and ended with sick dead-baby jokes. Warming up, her smile turns sly. "Not nearly so good as *Secrets of the Dead*."

"That's what you think," I say. But I concede, "Neither one is good as *Drop Dead Diva*."

"Oh no you didn't," Arden replies.

I snap at her. It's her turn, or she's out.

Scrambling, she snaps too, but it's more to stimulate her brain. She looks so pleased when she says, "You think they'll ever make *Shaun of the Dead* into a TV show?"

"No, but that movie *The Dead Zone* was good."

"I liked *Dawn of the Dead* better."

"*Evil Dead* was the best," I counter. Then I break the game when the best movie in the history of movies comes to mind. Technically it counts; it's part of the *Evil Dead* family. Way too excited, I slap the dashboard. "Oh man, *Army of Darkness*!"

"Shop smart!" Arden shouts, racking an imaginary shotgun.

I cry back, "Shop S-Mart!"

We can do this shit for hours.

# (OUTSIDERS)

**We take a cab into the suburbs to pick up the SUV. I** stand on the curb, because I've got nothing to add to the conversation Arden's trying to have.

All I am is the shotgun seat, here to (allegedly) keep her awake on the drive to Grand Junction. It's like a fifteen-hour drive; we have four days to get there. Even *I* could manage that.

However, Mr. Elliot—which is how this guy introduced himself, even though he looks to be in college at best—is walking back on the deal now that he's seen the two of us. Like most people, he doesn't say what he's thinking out loud. It's not flashing on a digital sign above his head or anything.

But I rolled out of the cab first, and you already know I look low-rent. Then comes Arden, fresh and high-end. Even though she wears a lot of black and white, it's always with prints, little embroidered stars, giant poppies, swirls and loops. Mr. Elliot actually pulled a double take, like he blinked, shook his head, and blinked again.

That's how the conversation got started, Mr. Elliot trying to confirm our identities, and Arden dancing so fast to prove it before he called her dad.

"I'm just really surprised that *you're* the courier," says Mr. Elliot. Then, he glances toward me again. Like I might try to boost his hubcaps while he's standing right there. The way he's sniffing, with his nostrils flared and his spine shock-straight—well, let's say I might have been willing to steal this car, just to piss him off.

Fortunately, Arden's in charge, and she's smooth. Assured and warm, she says, "I understand. This is your car, you're paying for this service. Trochessett & Tyler wants you to be a hundred and ten percent satisfied."

Supermodel Elliot (that's his job, I decide, he models high-end menswear and does photoshoots for cars and expensive liquor) says, "I'm glad you understand," and my heart sinks.

Just like the rental car that never was, we're about to lose out on a sweet Escalade because we're too fucking goofy to pull it off. If we're lucky, the Civic will be where we left it. I think it'll make it through Missouri and Kansas, maybe. They're flat states. The street-view ride through both of them shows mostly stubbled fields and asphalt stretching toward the horizon.

No way the Civic would make it through Colorado, though. Not mountains and valleys and shit. We'd try to get up the first incline, and it would be the little engine that tried and couldn't. But that's something to worry about tomorrow. The day after.

Arden pulls out her phone and starts messing with it. The little beeps seem to pierce my brain. A Dylan-whistle, straight into my ear. I know it's not turned up that loud. The frequency or the tone or something, it's painfully vivid. Not vivid, that's for colors. Audible, whatever, I don't know. My anxiety puts me right on the edge of hyperaware.

"Okay, good news," Arden says. "We can get someone else out here next Monday. We do have an express service. We'll put a new driver on the next flight to St. Louis."

Now Mr. Elliot frowns. "How much would that be?"

"Cost of the ticket—discounted, of course—give me a second,

I'll look it up in our travel database—"

Abruptly, Mr. Elliot says, "Let me see your driver's license again."

When Arden hands it over, Mr. Elliot studies it. He runs his fingers down the front, shuffles, then flips it over. I don't know what he thinks he's gonna find out looking at the reverse side. Who cares? He's obviously hemming. I understand. It's hard to walk away from a bargain.

She quoted him five hundred bucks; if he wants to bail on us, he's gonna pay a thousand plus airfare. I know what I'd pick. If I was in the business of hiring courier services to drive my cars for me, that is. Which I am. All the fucking time. I sit back in Village Estates, counting money, hiring couriers all day long. Last month, I shipped my Fabergé eggs to Gulfport, Mississippi, and back, just for the hell of it. Not my Monets, though; those I keep in the storage closet under the stairs.

I roll my eyes at myself; better than moaning. The tension is killing me, standing, listening, the wind in my hair, fuck, fuck, fuck, please just shut up and give us the fucking keys. C'mon, Mr. Elliot, you're rich, but rich people are still cheap bastards sometimes, right?

"You're fully insured?" Mr. Elliot asks, returning Arden's license.

"And bonded," Arden says. "It's the family business. My father wouldn't have it any other way."

Oh, glory, fuck me, hallelujah! The keys come out, and Mr. Elliot hands them to Arden like he's doing her a favor. Reluctantly, a little irritated, he produces green bills, counting them fast, then looking away. The dude's acting like he just paid for a hooker instead of a courier.

All charm, Arden reassures this guy that his SUV will make it to Grand Junction on time, without a scratch. I want to snatch Arden back, and whisper warnings right in her ear. Don't promise shit like that, come on! Doesn't she remember what happened when I said it would be fine if I drove from Cincinnati to Indianapolis? She's mocking the gods, predicting the future like that.

We're going to crash and die, I decide. Running new anxiety through my veins doesn't make me feel better. It adds, because if I haven't mentioned it, now that I'm not gonna die, I don't want to die. I don't want to go down into the dark. Maybe my life isn't much compared to other people's. No money, no prospects, probably just another future fry cook at the diner where my mother works, but damn it, it's *mine*.

"Are you okay?" Arden's voice startles me. It's suddenly in my ear. She's a ventriloquist, or she teleported.

Doesn't matter how she got from there to here so fast. Gathering up my stuff, I nod. "Let's go before he changes his mind."

"Seriously, are you okay? You look like you're going to pass out."

"I get anxious sometimes."

Arden drops a heavy hand on my shoulder and steers me toward the SUV. I open my own door, but she stands behind me until I climb in. This thing is terrifying; I ain't even lying. I'm sprawled in a leathery tomb; it's dark and humid until Arden climbs in, cranks it up and turns on the AC. Everything's too big. I feel like I found a Drink Me bottle, and now I'm rolling loose in this thing like a marble. A teeny, tiny flea. A grain of sand.

"I apologize for Kansas in advance," I say. This tank glides onto the road—I hear the tires at a distance, but it's nothing like the rattletrap the Civic was. It's even quieter than the Mercedes, and that was the choicest ride I ever been in. We bump over something and I clutch the seat belt. "But Colorado will be worth it."

As if to make sure that nobody should calm down too much, Arden's phone rings. Her dad's face springs up on the screen and I catch my breath. Shit. He knows. We got to St. Louis, but Arden went too far, breaking into the database. This was the smartest, stupidest plan in the world, and now we're caught.

Arden, though, answers like nothing's wrong at all—well, besides having to talk to her dad. She just punches the speaker button, because she's marooned in that driver's seat. Both of us are tiny in this thing, and it's almost ridiculous; I almost wanna know how her feet reach the pedals. They're reaching, though, because like clockwork, she rides the brakes and the Escalade shudders.

"Hey, David," Concrete Blocks says. His voice fills the SUV; it makes him physical in this space. "Hope I didn't wake you up."

"No," Arden replies. "I've been up awhile."

Concrete Blocks sounds distracted. "Good, good. Just making sure you got in all right."

And like before, Arden weaves a tale. She doesn't get snagged; there are no knots. Maybe she worked it all out in her head at some point. The way she talks to him about this imaginary spring break trip to my imaginary lake house, it's natural. She's so smooth, *I* almost believe her, and I know exactly where we are and what we're really doing.

"Hold on, I'm ordering," Concrete Blocks says. And then, he does. Arden and I exchange a look while we listen to her dad roll out his order at Starbucks. Once his something-whatever-double-don't-give-a-shit is getting made, he comes back. "David, are you still there?"

Arden presses two fingers to her temple, like she's got a head-ache starting. "I'm still here, Dad."

"Okay, good. I'm not gonna keep you. I just couldn't remember if I told you to put everything on the Amex."

"Because Mona's saving the miles to go to Cabo, yeah, you did."

Concrete Blocks starts talking to someone else—probably the cashier at his drive-thru now. It's just for a second, irritated at them, and then he tells Arden, "Right. All right, good. Get back to your friends. Don't do anything I wouldn't do."

"Never," Arden says.

Then she hangs up, the dark all around her again for a minute. I used to wish my mom would give half a shit. I wished that she would be one of those moms who checks in, comes to my door at night and watches me when I sleep. Tucks me up if a hand gets loose, stops by the hospital every day. Jokes with me, pretends like she's being cool when she's not, she's just not. I used to think if she was just *there*, I would feel better.

Arden's dad has checked on her every single day, and I'm pretty fucking sure she doesn't feel better.

# (1720.05)

**Kansas City is just a stop for gas and bottled water and** a car wash. When Arden promised Mr. Elliot spotless, she seriously meant it. There's a grey shell on the SUV. Soft, loose dust is crazy attracted to black paint, apparently. The car wash isn't one of those drive-through-and-drive-off jobbies. We stand in a glass hallway, watching as guys in damp clothes scrub every inch of the body clean.

Slipping up behind Arden—I sorta feel like I should be careful with her now—I rest my hand between her shoulder blades. It fits perfectly there, my thumb tracing one side, my pinkie, the other. Because there are strangers standing around next to us, I keep my voice low. "Sorry about your dad."

"Yeah, me too," Arden says, looking back. When she bites off her words, she all but spits them out. "It's like he knows when I'm happy. Or, even, when I just feel good. Comfortable. Whatever—it's like he knows, and that's exactly when he calls."

"Is there anything I can do?"

Arden turns her attention to the car again. The muscles in her shoulders twitch. "Nobody can do anything, Dylan. It's fine."

Is this quest making anything better for her? I think it's making things worse, actually. There's been some objectively shitty moments the last couple days, and I can admit it. I have regrets, okay? Part of me still wishes I could have been a better person, just left her alone. I sort of wish I had gone home and dragged my mother off the couch. Made her register me for school, even if she left right after.

But mostly what I regret is everything I've done to Arden, and everything I haven't. Maybe I should have kissed her in the cab. Maybe I should have kissed her in the morning; she wanted to. And I said no, because I had this idea. I said no, because quests are supposed to have destinations, and that felt like it should be one of them.

Only now, I'm thinking—maybe to her, it felt like rejection. I don't know what's rolling in her head right now; I know mine is full of back-and-forth, high-and-low. Mine's a mess, and I sort of assumed hers was as smooth and calm and quiet as her outside. But smooth and calm is how she lies. Quiet is how she stays close. Words from her lips.

I don't know how to do this. How to be close to her. To anybody. Since sixth grade, my life has been nothing but one side effect after another, one more step toward death, one more day closer to leaving everything behind. The news was never good. The bills were never paid. The end was never near enough.

They start to wish you'd die, and they do such a good job of covering it up and dressing it up and walking it around like it's sympathy.

—*Sometimes, Lynne. Sometimes I wish I would check on him and he'd be gone. Does that make me a monster?*

—*Girl, he's suffering. Wishing God would set him free from that, that's love, baby.*

—*I'm so damned tired.*

*—Who can blame you? I'm tired just watching you.*

I don't *think* they realized I could hear them through the vent in my room. But if they had, I wouldn't be shocked. Passive-aggressive is an art form with them. My mother and Lynne could win awards. That's what love was, for me. Listening to my mother and her best friend wishing I would just get on with it and die.

I'm doing this all wrong with Arden. And what's worse, I don't know how to do it right.

"You want me to leave you alone?" I ask Arden.

She stares through the glass, her reflection curved to meet her brow. For a long time, she doesn't say anything. But when I start to walk away, she catches my hand. Anchoring me, she still doesn't look over. "That number you called; they keep texting."

A black, bitter seed opens in my stomach. "Just block it."

"Is it your mom?" she asks. "It's your mom, right?"

Voice weighted, Arden trails off. There's a space there, I hear it. One where most people would say, *maybe you should call her.*

But Arden lets silence say it, because probably I think it's the last thing she wants to tell me.

Itty bitty Dylan wants to call. Itty bitty Dylan thinks that maybe this *one* time, Mom'll be glad to hear from me. I've been gone five days; she has no idea where I am. But my mother is an actress. She sees drama; she dives into it. If she had the chance, she might have an affair with a really old guy, just to have the chance to throw herself on his casket in front of his legitimate family. Her whole life has been a performance.

It's my turn to talk, so I say, "Yeah, but it's not for me. She thinks your number is one of her boyfriends."

"Oh," Arden says.

"He owes her money," I add. "Two hundred bucks."

A shadow crosses Arden's face. She doesn't free my hand. As she moves down to watch the Escalade progress through the car wash, she tugs me along. "Who cares that much about two hundred dollars?"

"That's a *lot* where I come from."

Finally, she faces me. Pulls a little, so I'm in her orbit. Right there in the middle of a car wash, she asks, "What are we doing here, Dylan?"

It feels like she punched me. Dead center, cracking my bones and pressing all my air out. The pain radiates, a web that reaches the tips of my fingers, the curl of my toes. "We're going on a quest. We're finding the Pearl Ship."

She pauses, then she looks at me. "Am I just your ride?"

Those words land with a sting, the whip-snap of a scorpion right through my chest. It's my fault they land, my fault it hurts. I let myself love her—selfishly, fine. Badly, whatever, but I love her, and she thinks that about me.

And what's worse is, she could be right. I've ruminated over every way I ruined her; made myself sick thinking about all the things I been taking from her; talked myself out of feeling guilty for the things I still want.

Even though her laugh makes me new, and the sound of her voice telling stories is the sweetest song I've ever heard—I could have been lying to us both all along. I don't think so; I don't believe that. I don't . . . but now maybe Arden does.

So brittle, so breakable, I draw back, pulling my hand out of hers. I don't know what to say; I don't trust myself to get it right, so I back toward the door, far away from her. I say, "I need some air."

Then I turn and push into the sunshine and let it burn me up.

# (IT GETS DARK SOON)

**Tense silence slows the road. I roll around loose in my** oversized navigator's seat. We're into the nothing, now. Hand to god, just nothing. Road and road signs and empty fields. No, wait, there's a couple of scrubby trees. Almost hills that rise and fall like waves. Don't get too excited, a cell phone tower in the distance.

When we pass some cut stone on the side of the road, it's stained dusty red and weak green. Red from clay I guess, green from the crap growing right off the side of it.

This landscape is lonely, and it hones the tension in the car. Even if I wanted to reach out to Arden, she's all the way over on the other side. There's two seats' worth of space between us.

Maybe that's just how rich people roll. They want their own world, and nobody in it. Or maybe they're worried that the rest of us just want to cut off a slice.

Either way, I can't reach her. She doesn't want to reach me.

This time, I don't know if I owe her an apology, or if she owes me one. So I do what's easy. I ball my hoodie up and use it for a pillow. I lean against the glass, and close my eyes and drift away.

# (1465.77)

**When I wake up, we're on a highway instead of the inter-**state. It's two-lane, the kind that slows through little towns, and heads into the heart of nowhere. Rubbing my face, I try to orient myself, but it's impossible. I don't know which way we're headed—I don't even know when we left 70.

Everywhere, I hurt. A different kind of pain. I knew how to be sick; I knew how to bitch about dead nerves and sick stomachs. The skull-splitting headaches, and the grinding of my bones, it was agony. It wasn't something I got used to. But that kind of pain makes sense, so much more sense than *this*. This, right now, I'm empty in my own skin, like everything that mattered got gored out and thrown away. Finally, I lift my head in search of water. There's a bottle in the console, and I reach for it.

"Morning, sunshine," Arden says.

It's not morning; it's nowhere near. Uncapping the water, I take a swallow and try not to look at her. "Where are we?"

"Just a detour," Arden says, "I already checked. If we stay on this, we'll end up back on 70 in a couple hours."

"Did we go way out of the way?" I ask.

"Not too far."

This is just like hitching a ride to Columbus and ending up in Cincinnati instead. Maybe my plan wasn't a good one, but it was all I had. From where we picked up the car, the Salton Sea is twenty-seven hours away. But that's if we drive it strict. That's if we find a car right away when we have to drop this one off in Grand Junction. That's if Arden still wants to go.

I choke myself with another big swallow of water. Being hollow hurts enough; I don't want to fill myself up with tears.

Arden says, "I need to stop soon. I'm getting road hypnosis."

For a second, I think about asking her to let me drive, but I know she won't. And she probably shouldn't, seeing as how it's her ass on the line with this car. The last time she let me drive, I got us pulled over, and I pushed a little knife beneath her skin. Maybe that was the day she started to doubt me. That's a thought I can't have, I can't, I won't. I pull my bag into my lap, but nothing in it rattles.

Steadying myself, I ask, "Is there even anywhere out here to stop?"

It's a fair question. There are more trees now. And stick-and-plumb towns, too. (You stick your head out the window, you're plumb outta town.) No hotels I've seen—to be fair, I've been asleep for a while and barely awake five minutes. Somehow, I have a feeling if we find somewhere to stay, it's going to be Baytes-like. I don't think Arden will trust this SUV to another motel like that.

Assured, Arden says, "We'll find something."

Looking into the back, I wonder out loud, "Do the seats lay out? If we can find a rest stop, we can just sleep in here."

There's nothing left in my bag, but I find the last of my Tic Tacs laying on the floor between my feet. Those, I pluck up. Just to feel the memory, I shake the bottle. A couple mints fall into my hand and I swallow them like pills. I turn to Arden; I offer the box. "You want one?"

She doesn't; she just waves them away. I can't make her out. I can't tell what this serenity is. Has she made up her mind about me? Does she have a next step, and is she going to be like, smooth and practiced, until we get to the point where she leaves me behind? She said she might not go home; there's no reason why she can't keep going without me.

My face starts to get hot, so I turn the AC vents at me. Tucking my arms behind my head, I shiver but I don't move. After a minute just looking at the road, I see why Arden needs a break.

The lines streak beneath our wheels, the shoulders blur to white. A low, soft hum surrounds us. It's peaceful, and peaceful's not really where you wanna be when you're in charge of a couple tons of steel. And right now, Arden's in charge, with lines elegantly sculpted into her brow.

It ruins the curve of her profile. I wonder if this trip has ruined her. If it's breaking her—or pushing her to an edge she already saw coming.

"You aren't just my ride," I tell her.

Arden doesn't say anything right away. Her body shapes around her thoughts, though. Her shoulders roll slightly; her lips part.

"You know how you keep saying you've never done stuff? Never seen stuff?"

"Yeah."

"I have," she says. Shaking herself out, she realigns herself behind the wheel—proof she's getting tired. "I've been to Europe. I've been to the Bahamas. LA and New York and Miami . . . Disneyland, King's Island. Camped in the mountains. Stayed at a beach house, swum in the ocean . . ."

"Walked on Mars," I say softly.

"Yeah."

"So . . . what? Just adding a pin to your map?"

Dragging her lower lip through her teeth, Arden draws a breath. Holds it. Then she exhales and looks to me. "I don't really remember any of it. I went because my parents went. My friends went. I *went along*. It didn't matter if I did; the trip would have been the same with or without me.

"You said, let's go. And I realized if I didn't . . . you wouldn't." She smiles crookedly. "I don't know what this is, exactly. It's obviously *crazy*. But it's mine. And yours. It's ours."

"Yeah it is," I say, and now my throat closes completely. It's just like all those trips we took in the game. Didn't make a difference to the world or the people around us if we walked from one end of the continent to the other. It only made a difference for us. Straightening myself out, I say, "You're right."

"About what?"

"This wouldn't be happening if it weren't for you. I don't quest without you, you know that."

"It's dangerous to go alone," she jokes. "Take Arden."

The shadows start to fade. And then, Arden steps on the brakes again. The belt locks against my chest; that almost startles me more than anything. But when I look out, I realize we've driven into a town. Tired buildings spring up on either side of the road. With barely a nudge, Arden steers into a parallel parking spot and drops it out of gear. Plucking the keys from the ignition, she unlocks the doors. "Come on."

Bathroom break? I can't see where. Everything looks like it's closed. Not because it's after hours. It's not even sunset yet. They just have handpainted signs in the windows: Closed, Closed, Closed.

There's nothing here. It's a broken-down bit of Middle America, nothing to recommend it.

She waits for me at the hood ornament, then slides an arm around my shoulders. Once I'm beside her, she turns. Her nose brushes my hair, her warm breath teasing my ear. To me, into me, she whispers, "I told you it was in Kansas."

There, across the street, in a rust-roofed shelter, is the World's Largest Ball of Twine.

It sits in a semi-vacant lot, a yellow brick building behind it. The Cawker City water tower shines in the background, a beacon above several half-demolished buildings. The sign on the brick wall says the ball was forty foot three inches in 1988, and fourteen thousand six hundred eighty-seven pounds.

And even though this ball of twine's not exactly round, and it's framed by concrete benches and pillars, and it's standing on the dying Main Street of a dwindling town, it's fucking beautiful. It's golden and massive and perfect. My chin quivers and my throat tightens. This is the stupidest thing I've ever seen in my life, and I love it.

I love *her*.

Suddenly, Arden wraps around me. Arms around me, brow against mine. A shield against the world, saving me from a roadside attraction. She's murmuring, "Don't cry. Dylan come on, don't cry, I thought you'd like it."

Then she's not saying anything at all, because I kiss her. I'm too tired to lift my arms, to wrap them around her neck. So I twist my fingers in the front of her shirt instead. I pull her down. Her heat spills into me, and my heart races. It might be a little misshapen, it might taste like salt and Mountain Dew, but I'm lost in her kiss all the same.

Trembling against her, I break away to catch my breath then rush for another taste. Her mouth is just as soft as it looks; it's liquid fire. Each caress feeds heat to my veins, and I cling until we're both dizzy and we both draw back. Her eyes are so wide; my lips are so swollen.

Most people don't realize when they've had their last first kiss. Now I don't either. This might be the last, or the first of a thousand, and it's fucking amazing to know that I don't know. All that matters is that this one, this first, belongs to Arden.

She makes time stop.

# (WEBSTER STATE PARK)

**We're too far off the main drag to find a motel, so we go** down Highway 24 awhile and end up paying to camp at a park. The ranger at the gate tries to tell us the good outlook spots, but it's not like we're setting up a tent and taking in the view. Arden listens to the directions, and then just takes the first camping spot we find.

It's kind of desolate out here, early in the year for camping, apparently. Bare trees whisper around us, bare limbs whipping in the wind. According to the park map, there's a lake nearby. If I stop and listen, completely still, I hear the waves.

It turns out in *new* cars, there's a manual. Arden pulls it from the glove box, flipping through it. Pressing close behind her, all I do is distract her. My arms loop around her waist; I cling while she searches for the instructions to the backseats. When she wriggles free, I stick out my lower lip and get rewarded with a kiss. I make a mental note: remember that trick for later.

After some folding, and some cussing, and actually, some more kissing up against the side of the Escalade, we figure out how to fold the seats. They make something like a bed to crash in, slippery because they're leather, cold for the same reason. For a lumpy pillow, we have the bag with our clothes in it; my hoodie and her jacket are pretty thin for blankets.

But who needs a blanket, really? *Arden* is my heat. My restless hands chase her bare skin. Her arms; I can touch her arms as I steal another taste of her mouth—her face, her cheeks: they burn beneath my fingers. When I get my hands into her hair, I get tangled. All those curls lace me up and it's awkward. But Arden laughs softly, right against my lips. She steals the kiss from me and slips past my lips, and somehow manages to free me all at the same time.

There's a good chance, a real good chance, that I'm bad at this. A wavery beat runs up and down my spine; it's a pulse that flickers through my chest, uncertain, uneven. My breath is thin; it's loud. It fills up the Escalade. And it's a true fact, it turns out to be a true fact, that tangling and twining and kissing and touching in the dark, it fogs glass windows right up.

Ever since I stepped in Arden's room, her scent has haunted me. Now I'm alive in it, pressing my face against the curve of her neck, breathing her in. When she streaks a hand beneath my shirt, I catch my breath. Her touch is a trail of heat, and my heart pounds. I'm lit up; I feel like I'm sending up sparks, not a warning—a call. *Yes, there, and there*—and then the sparks flicker out when she finds the scar from my PICC line.

Measuring it with her touch, she pushes up on an elbow and kisses it through my shirt. Sparks again; sparks everywhere, and now we're peeling off shirts to get to skin. Just like her hands, her chest is winter gold— in the dark, it catches our little light, it seems to glow. Her bra cracks when I catch fingers in it, but the way it falls away, I think it was supposed to unfasten like that. I hope so. If I broke it, I'm sorry and I kiss the middle of her chest to apologize.

She pulls my hand to the dark, flat curve of her nipple, and presses her own to mine. What little experience I have was rush and hurry: rough, hard kisses to distract from the fact that it's awkward to yank open your clothes in a hydrotherapy bed. Nobody's touched me like this before, like Arden does. I follow her. Every touch, I follow her. I find her in the taste of her skin. I find her in the arch of her back as she settles beneath me. I find her in the sound she makes when I rasp my thumb across her navel.

She spills out beneath me as my palm skims the hitching flat of her belly. This time, *she* hesitates. And this time, I'm not scared, because she wasn't scared of me. Her breath comes in soft whispers and I like the fact that leggings come off easier than jeans. My jeans, I have to roll to the side and fight with them. Probably I look like a jackass, and I don't care. When I finally kick them free, I roll into her again and we collide with a kiss.

My knee presses between hers; her thighs are silk parting to mine. Sliding together, our bodies grind in a long, slow caress. I feel her everywhere beneath me. She rises and falls, elemental. She's thunder in the distance; she's a storm on my lips. Her pale hand drifts in the dark, down to adjust her body the way she wants it. When she smooths her sac out of the way, I glide in to press my thigh tight beneath it.

There's a soft spot there; I know when I find it because her whole body shudders. Pressed tight between our bodies, my erection stings and swells. It's almost painful—rocking against her is the only thing that takes the edge off. There's a rhythm here, both of us trying to find it. At first, it's off—like we both missed the bass drop.

But she plays a hand down my back; I trace my fingers into her hair. We hold our breath at the same time, and then I smile. I realize probably nobody knows what they're doing—not in the dark for the first time, not when they look out at the horizon and have to figure out how to get there. What I know is, I want to write her name into my skin; I want to keep her always.

Brushing my nose against hers, I murmur, "Okay?"

She exhales; her lips curve on mine and she nods.

Together, we find the beat.

# (TWO THiNGS)

**After our skins dry and our sweat cools, it's cold in the**
Escalade. At first, we scramble around trying to piece together
something to cover us. Then I remember that space blanket I
took when I dumped my mother's car at the gas station. Covering up with it is like getting rolled in tinfoil. When I tug Arden
into the curve of my arm, the blanket *crackles*. Arden giggles.

There's a lot more giggling as we try to settle in. Eventually we
fade down to quiet, pressed between soft kisses that are more
warmth than shape. Sleep flickers in and out; once, she jolts
awake again, pushing up to look at me. There's all this wonder
in her eyes, and I have no idea why she likes looking at me. All
I know is I'm not gonna argue it.

"What are you thinking?" she asks, just as I start to drift off.

Warmth spreads through me and I tug her closer. "That I didn't expect this."

"Me either." She burrows closer, weaving her ankle between mine. For a long time, she doesn't say anything. The air around us is just quiet and full; she presses her fingertips into my chest, one after the other. It's an idle touch, almost incidental, like her breath across my skin. Then she kisses my collarbone and says, "You know what's been amazing about this quest?"

She doesn't want my answer, though. She buries her face against my neck and goes on before I can say a word. "I wake up and get dressed, and you don't say, *is that what you're wearing?* I put on lip gloss, I don't, whatever, it doesn't matter. You roll over, you say, 'Morning, Arden.'"

"'Cause there you are," I reply.

"There I am," she agrees. "I want that from everybody. I want the world to say, 'Good morning, Arden!' with a smile. I want people to meet me and shake my hand, and whatever they notice is different, is different, and who cares? People are afraid to touch me, sometimes, you know that? You're not."

Furrowing my brow, I try to look down at her. She's hidden behind her hair; even when I try to brush it out of the way it springs back. "What's to be afraid of?"

"That's what I want to know." She shifts, stealing a look at me. "My mother wasn't. I mean, she actually understood, you know? I told her when I was seven; I told her when I was young enough to get hormone blockers, and she understood. She bought me the clothes I needed, and told the school she would sue them to next Sunday if they had a problem with it."

There's a question right there on my lips; I weigh it, but I ask. "Then what the hell happened?"

"She wouldn't stand up to my Dad." Arden stirs, raising her head. She stares past me though, spilling this out like she needs to exorcise it. "He was always, 'This is a phase.' Then for a while, he was just like, 'David's gay; he's confused, he'll figure it out.' And then all, 'What if he changes his mind?' He didn't want me to do anything *permanent*, just in case.

"So I'm six feet tall and built like a rugby player, and you know what? I'm okay with that now. I wish it was easier to find clothes that fit, but I'm not trying to *hide*. If there's a little Arden on the street somewhere, I want her to look at me and see herself, you know?"

"I know," I murmur. I roll my head toward her and just drink her in. There's so much passion in her, so much light—I don't look away. I want to be blinded.

"So that's what's been amazing about this quest." All at once she blushes. Her voice gets softer and her shoulders go round. This time, when she looks at me, it's almost shy. "One of the things."

I feel like a king, 'cause there's two.

# (1085.57)

**In the morning, early, we take another slice through** fields and grain and endless skies, then we're back at I-70, which looks exactly the same. Trying to make up some time, we drive and drive until the low-fuel light kicks on and we have no choice. We've made it almost to Denver when we coast into a truck stop on fumes.

I fill the SUV while Arden ducks inside. I cannot fucking believe how much money just went into this gas tank; maybe we shoulda bought a car with premium unleaded instead of OxyContin, damn.

When Arden's not back by the time I finish at the pump, I head inside. Skulking through the racks of random crap for sale, I finally find Arden at the ATM. For laughs, I grab a ball cap from a rack and pull it on. With quiet steps, I creep up behind her and she startles when I slip my arms around her waist. Everything is new with her. A few kisses, a long night sleeping next to her, and I feel a little drunk. A little goofy, and I savor it.

With my chin resting on her shoulder, I watch as she slips one card, then another, into the slot. "Whatcha doing?"

"Stuff," she replies. She clutches a fold of bills, shooting me a smile between transactions. "You want that hat?"

"No, it's ugly."

She makes the ATM perform, singing all kinds of notes, spitting out all kinds of money. When she finally tucks the last card and the roll into her wallet, she's carrying something like five thousand dollars. Five thousand. Plucked out of the ether, guarded by plastic cards. I can't even wrap my head around that.

"They don't have my bank out here," she says with a sigh. "I asked."

Under my breath, I fall into step with her and murmur, "So you robbed an ATM?"

"Cash advances," she explains.

May as well talk Swahili at me. I understand how paycheck loan places work, but getting money you don't have out of a bank machine? Sorry, no convincing me that's not some kind of magic. And why not? Arden makes all things possible.

Nobody tackles us as we walk out (I leave the hat at the counter), and we make it all the way back to the SUV before I have to ask. Flailing in my seat, I can't contain myself. If spending three hundred bucks on a credit card at Walmart was something, four figures of actual cash is insane. It's play money because nobody has money like that just in their wallet.

"What for? We're getting paid, right?"

"Not enough. The last time we tried to buy a car from the lot, they wouldn't take my card." Arden shrugs, carefully backing out of the parking space. "Everybody takes cash."

I stare at her. "And the credit card just *gives* it to you?"

"No, I have to pay it back. It'll show up on the bill."

The closest I ever seen to turning cards into money is people trading their EBT for cash. And that's a personal transaction, under the table, where nobody's watching. What Arden just did, that's high-class mob shit as far as I'm concerned. I never even seen that much money at once.

The petty hoods I know pretend they're loaded, carrying a single hundred dollar bill, wrapped around a wad of ones. Arden's roll is twenties on top of twenties as far as the eye can see. That's real. That's *terrifying*. Settling next to her, I say, "You're like the mafia or something."

Her laughter rings out. "Oh yeah, I'm hardcore."

# (WORST MONUMENT, F---, WOULD NOT DRIVE AGAIN)

**For the most part, Arden lets me sleep when I sleep. And** the thing is, I don't *mean* to keep dropping off. But my body doesn't know how to go this long or this hard. Yeah, mostly it's riding in cars. Sometimes it's walking. Sometimes, like last night, it's reaching out and touching the sky like I'm a thousand feet tall.

All of it, it's a lot and I'm mostly used to laying in bed. So I'm tired, and I nod off, and Arden lets me. That's why it surprises me when she shakes me. It's not gentle either, and part of the reason I open my eyes is because I'm afraid she's going to progress to face-slapping.

That's what the movies tell you to do if somebody won't wake up. I'm not sure how *effective* it is, but I don't need to find that out personally.

"Dylan," she says. "You awake?"

"Yeah." I swallow and turn my face away because I can smell my own breath. She doesn't need to get a whiff. Struggling to sit up, I realize that at some point, she put my seat all the way back. Sometimes I think the two of us are taking very different trips to the Salton Sea. We just keep meeting up in the middle of it.

"We're getting ready to hit the big tunnel. I thought you might want to see it."

I rub a hand down my face and look outside. Mountains, fuck me, there are *mountains*. Suddenly mountains, everywhere. Green and stretching away into clouds, trees and valleys. This is what I've been waiting for, brand-new mountains. Because I'm almost civilized, I don't plaster my hands to the windows when I look out, but I want to.

The Appalachians are round and soft, a gajillion years old. Those, I grew up with and they bore me to tears. But the Rockies, these babies are proud and just out of the box, only about a bazillion years old. (I don't remember the dates, sorry. You can look 'em up.) They're beautiful; they fill me up, just looking at them.

"When did this happen?" I ask breathlessly, rolling down my window.

"What?" Arden asks.

"The mountains."

"The last twenty minutes or so," Arden tells me. "You weren't asleep that long."

The air outside isn't particularly sweet. It smells like the side of a highway: hot oil, gravel, gasoline, dead grass. I don't care. In my mind, it smells like Christmas trees. It feels like cool breezes; there's no snow, I realize. Maybe farther west, maybe just not yet. I really want to see snow again.

Two beige, industrial mouths gape open. On the right side, it gobbles cars and semis and motorcycles alike. On the left, it vomits them out in a steady stream. Over the swallowing mouth, slender letters spell out EISENHOWER TUNNEL 1973.

"We're going to drive under the Continental Divide," she says, shooting me a smile. Even though the SUV is an automatic, the gears hum like they want to shift. The ride is smooth-smooth-smooth, but gravity pulls. We're climbing mountains the Trochessett Way: leather seats, tinted windows, full-speed ahead.

Raising my seat, I lean forward. My heart thunders. It skitters to a stop when we actually drive inside.

The tunnel is claustrophobic. It's like the inside of a kiln or a crypt and oh my god, I hate this. Tile the shade of a smoker's teeth stretches beside us, and over. Lights line the ceiling, flickering just enough to play hell in my eyes. Green arrows point out the lanes, because it's darkish in here. And loud. It's so loud, like a swarm of locusts. It's like a fucking MRI, and here I am, trapped and helpless again and shit. The other cars are too close; we're going too fast.

Clutching the armrest, I bite my lips to keep them closed. This is when I realize we're still going up. I feel the pull, even though the SUV doesn't struggle at all. It glides smoothly through this hellmouth. I barely see the sign that says Continental Divide; it's just a vertical strip on the wall. It flashes past; it gives way to the digital sign dangling from the ceiling.

It doesn't say welcome or have a nice day or any good thing, it's a warning. We're going down now, speeding impossibly fast in this impossibly tiny tunnel and the sign yells at truckers. *Use the right brakes! All downhill from here, motherfuckers! Don't crash!* I can't even breathe to wheeze. All I can do is press my back against the seat and wait for it to be over.

I'm laced with so much anxiety, I can't even cry. It's like every single bit of me tightened into a knot. My mind is blank, my lips are numb, and I stare.

Idly, Arden says, "I never liked tunnels myself."

She's so good, her eyes are on the road. She doesn't know I'm flipping my shit. I'm glad; she'd feel bad if she realized she woke me up just for me to end up pissing myself. She'd take that hard. Inside, I tell myself: *It won't last long; I'll be okay. Tunnels end, they do, they have to, because there are* warnings *for the trucks as we careen out of the tunnel and into the sunlight again.*

And then, I breathe.

The whole sky opens up, the mountains cradling us, the sun pouring down. We're in the sky, and now the speed feels like we're breaking free. Choking on my relief, I drag my fingers through my hair. The strands burn my skin and I hold out my hand. It trembles; it's a seismograph measuring my anxiety.

What's weird is that right now, I feel . . . good. All that panic turned to joy. Arden sits next to me, and she's beautiful. When she catches me looking, she smiles. For me, just for me.

# (NOT EXACTLY A ROAD CONVERSATION)

**It's gonna be a rest stop for us tonight. Already we** proved we can sleep in this thing (and then some), but it turns out, only real well when it's dark and quiet. All around us, cars pull in; they pull out.

They talk by our windows. They make the Escalade shake when they slam their doors. I'm in-and-out awake, and so is Arden. Somewhere in the middle of the night, she wakes me up laughing.

It's creepy, I ain't gonna lie. She's just laying there next to me, laughing. Carefully, I give her a shove. (I hope something nightmare ain't about to happen; if she opens her eyes and there's nothing there, I'm gonna ruin these expensive, expensive seats.)

"Sorry," Arden says, and jesus, thank god, her eyes are just eyes.

With another nudge, I ask her, "What's so funny?"

At first, I think she's pretending to go back to sleep on me. But then, her laughter rises up again. Throwing an arm over me, she pushes up to peer at me in the dark. "Too slow!"

Baffled, I stare at her. "What?!"

"You drive *too slow*," she cackles, then slumps on my chest.

So in the middle of the night, in Colorado, days away from Ohio, Arden's losing her shit *now* because I got us pulled over *then*. The lack of sleep has got her goofy or something, and I drop a hand on the back of her neck. She's warm and shaking against me. It's a good sound; out of place as all get out, but so what? She deserves to laugh.

That doesn't mean she gets to mock me, though. Stroking her back, I say, "You're drunk, Arden, go home."

At that, she dissolves into fresh laughter. In the dark, she clings to me, and she giggles and what the hell can I do? Nothing. Not a thing. So I hold her until she starts to fall asleep again. Just when I'm about to fall off too, she raises her head once more.

"From here on out," she announces, "I'm calling you Slo-Mo. Slo-Mo Stefansky."

"Terror of the Interstate," I agree, rolling my eyes.

That only makes her laugh more.

# (PUSH)

**The road is especially urgent now. It's all downhill, liter-**
ally. We have to fight to slow down instead of struggling to
speed up. It's racing, whether we want to or not, through a
paved valley cloaked in evergreen.

I've been on Arden's phone for a while, searching for used cars
online. We're going to need one, soon. I consider the motorcycles wistfully, but let's be honest: I'd fall asleep and fall right
the fuck off. Whatever we buy next, it's going to have seats and
walls and a roof. And belts. Hopefully floors.

"How far now?" I ask when I look up, because I know she's
keeping track.

Pretty when she purses her lips, Arden says, "Well, that depends. Do you want to spend the night in the desert, or . . ."

The way she says it tells me she has a plan. I think it doesn't matter if I want to spend the night among the sand and the cactus. (Maybe I do, maybe I don't. There are wolves and coyotes and snakes and scorpions in the desert, right? Maybe not wolves. I think wolves like trees. Or do they just live near them? Are wolves even real anymore outside zoos? Shit. I just lost my train of thought.)

Oh, I know where I was going:

It's nice to see her picking and deciding. She's earned that; she doesn't have to be quiet. She shouldn't want to be invisible. And me, I've been needing to learn to just let things happen, too. If I give it up to her, it's good. If she takes it and runs, that's good. We're both good. And I slipped into the secret lives of lupines instead of filling in the end of her sentence like I was supposed to.

"Or?" I ask.

"Vegas, baby!"

Suddenly, Arden dances behind the wheel. Her spine is liquid; even seated, her hips sway. That is, honest to god, the sexiest thing I've ever seen in my life. All her lines animate. She's beautiful, stretched out with her winter gold skin and dark brown hair. Her curls bounce as she twists her fingers together, pumping her arms above the wheel.

When I don't say anything (or join in, probably), Arden gets self-conscious, and stops. "What?"

Unexpectedly honest, I say, "I was just enjoying the show."

She blushes. Her sweet, sweet face turns pink, and she looks back at the road. It makes me crazy that she keeps hiding that. That the world expects her to hide that.

"Anyway," she says. "If we pushed to ten hours on the road today, we could make it to Vegas by nightfall. I think. I mean, if we find a car fairly quickly."

Holding up her phone, I say, "We're going to drive right past Westward Ho Used Cars. Two thousand two Saturn sedan, four thousand bucks, out the door."

"No kidding?" she asks.

"It's green," I say, then do a little dance of my own. Arms above my head, just for a few bounces. "Like your eyes."

She asks, "Are you flirting with me?"

"I'm always flirting with you."

# (840.82)

**Grand Junction isn't an exit. It appears on the highway,** blooming up trailers and gas stations on either side of the divide. It seems a strange place to take a high-ticket SUV, but whatever. Ours is not to question why and all that. We stop first at the car lot, to buy us the ship that will sail us to the Salton Sea.

The entire time we sit in that over-ACed office, I tremble. Not because it's cold, or because I'm sick. But because we're almost there. Way back in Ohio, Colorado was ephemeral. A wraith of a state, not yet real. It's real now, all these places are real. I feel small among new mountains. They were here before people ever were. They'll be around when we're gone. Next to the Rockies, we're all a blink of the eye.

I stare at them as Arden signs paperwork. Westward Ho sells us the Saturn with no problem at all. She proves she has insurance by pulling it up online, and they're all good with that, and fine and dandy, papers signed, let's go to VEGAS, BABY! Well, let's let me follow behind Arden in the new car, while she drops off the Escalade.

Leaving it behind, I have to take one long, last look. It was too big, too expensive, too everything. But it's got one of my best memories in it, so I have to say good-bye. Good-bye SUV, good-bye Colorado, and soon, good-bye I-70.

We don't even turn left. Not really.

The highway arches in a long curve, we merge, and then we're heading south. There were no signs. No notice, no little historical marker: now leaving the fifth largest transcontinental highway in the United States. We're on it, then we're not, and the pavement's smooth as can be. The only difference is that the mountains are on my arm now, instead of at the tip of my nose.

When Arden's phone rings, I touch the buttons and turn on speaker for her, but say nothing. I've been clutching the phone for a while now. I was taking pictures when one highway turned into the next, and I just never put it back down.

"How's the lake?" Arden's father asks. His voice is in my hands; I stare at the screen. There's an icon of a bomb with a smiley face on it instead of a picture. Concrete Blocks sounds just the same as ever. Which is to say, not friendly, not anything. Just stiff.

With the same practiced exhaustion, Arden lies, "Cold, and maybe I'm crazy, but I think the mosquitos are out early."

"I wasn't aware they had mosquitos in Grand Junction, Colorado. You learn something new every day."

Arden mouths, "Great," and she reaches for the phone. Wedging it between her thumb and her forefinger, she presses it against the wheel. The needle on the speedometer rises, tick, tick, tick. It's okay, we were going about five under so we can stand to pick up some speed. Steeling herself, Arden says, "They have mosquitos everywhere, Dad."

Plastering a hand over my mouth, I don't laugh out loud. I don't make a sound. But that was a fine clapback; I'm so proud of her. The Jedi mind trick comes back, a full, vivid memory, and that underlines it for me: this guy is a dick. He doesn't know anything about his daughter. Oh yeah, Arden just fired a barb at Concrete Blocks, and I'm going to celebrate it for her.

"The insurance company called," Concrete Blocks says. "There's a problem with the VIN number on the car you bought. It might be stolen. Or perhaps the lien didn't come off when the previous owner paid it off. It's hard to say."

"Can you take care of that?" Arden asks.

Holy shit, she's not just mouthing off to him. She's standing up. Maybe for the first time ever. Instead of scared, she sounds certain. When she straightens her shoulders this time, it's with authority. I don't know what happened; I don't know what changed. But Arden's pushing back and it's beautiful.

"I'm not amused, David. Why are you in Colorado?"

Changing lanes, Arden lifts her chin. "I'm taking a friend to California."

"Where's *your* car?"

Heavy silence sinks around us, and Arden finally says, "It got stolen in Ohio."

Concrete Blocks' voice never rises. It's a cool, clean dagger edge, cutting through the distance. "You're driving to the next airport and coming home immediately. Where are you?"

"I told you. I'm taking a friend to California," Arden repeats.

There's a quaver in her voice. She's not invisible at all right now. I rub her thigh because her hands are busy. It's all I can do, but it's a marvel and a horror to watch. I feel like I shouldn't be listening, but I can't help but devour every word.

"There will be a one-way ticket for you at the Delta counter in Las Vegas. I suggest you get on the plane, David."

"*David* won't be there," Arden says. Her courage falters; her voice falls nearly to a whisper. "*David's* not coming back."

There's a pause. Concrete Blocks loses some of his cool. The edge crumbles and he says, "I canceled the insurance. I canceled your credit cards. There's a hold on your bank account. I'm reporting the car stolen, and reporting you missing."

Damn. Damn it, damn. Daddy snaps back. I start to sweat, a bitter, anxious sheen that leaves me oily and probably pungent. I don't know what happens now. Concrete Blocks has connections. He's not afraid to call the cops; there are consequences and dangers untold, and what did I get Arden into?

Squeezing Arden's knee, I mouth to her, "I don't want to fuck up your life."

Her eyes flash. She tells her father, "I have to get going."

Out loud, I finally murmur. I beg, a halo around my god-damned head, I can be good. I can fix things instead of ruin them. "Just leave me in Las Vegas, Arden. I'll hitchhike to California."

"Who is that?" Concrete Blocks demands.

"That's the friend," Arden says. "Bye, Dad."

She tries a couple of times to hang up. Her hands aren't steady enough so I take the phone from her. I tap the screen, I end the call. Then I dig around in the settings to turn the thing on airplane mode. It's not like it will stop Arden from putting it back later. But she won't have to get nine thousand million calls from the evilest man in the world in the meantime.

"It's really okay," I say. "It's a miracle we made it this far."

Reserve breaking, Arden raises her voice. "Goddamn it, Dylan, we're four hours away. When we stop for the night, we're going to be four hours away from the Salton Sea, all right? I want to see it. Maybe that makes me a bitch, but I came this far and *I* want to see it."

"Well fuck you," I say, trying to jolt or jolly her out of it. "I wanted to see it first."

"Fuck you," she replies softly.

"You wouldn't even know about it if it weren't for me." I take off my seat belt, because really, what's the worst that can happen? (Don't answer that.) I slide closer to her, wrapping an arm around her waist. I press my face into the clean warmth of her arm, and I kiss the curve of her shoulder. It's getting dark outside, actually dark. We've spent nights together, but this is our third night, *together*.

Some of her ice melts. Turning her head quickly, she kisses my brow and then looks back at the highway. "Yeah, well, you wouldn't have gotten here without me."

I kiss her again, her ear, the little spot that's so soft behind it. Her shoulder; I pull her hand to my lips and kiss her fingers, too. When she peeks my away again, I kiss her knuckles and I tell her the truth, the truest thing ever.

"And don't think I'll ever forget that, either."

# (333.80)

**If you pay in cash, nobody in Vegas cares who you are.**

With the leftover from the car, and the money for delivering the Escalade, Arden decides we're staying in a suite that overlooks the whole city. From every direction, the elevator reflects us. It's funhouse time, with rivets in our faces and our bodies stretched out wide. Neither of us looks like ourselves; that's fair.

My ears pop halfway up, and sound roars into my head. I hear gears grinding, and people laughing. Machinery hums; Arden's keys jingle as she shakes them anxiously. On other floors that we pass, other elevators ding. We had to slide our key card to even push the button for our floor.

When the elevator stops, I see why. It opens into a palace. Our shoes scrape across marble, then shuffle on smooth, camel carpet. There's ocean-blue chairs and a creamy silk bed. A dining room, a desk—right off to the side, a bathroom with a tub as big as a Jacuzzi.

Fuck, it's so rich. At first, I'm afraid to walk in. I feel like I should take off my shoes, maybe scrub myself off before I touch any of this stuff. It overwhelms me, all this luxury. I'm so small inside it; I don't belong. Arden smooths her warm hands over my shoulders, and my anxiety melts. She kisses my hair, and all my joints loosen. I'm safe here; I'm with her.

So I let my bag slip from my shoulder, and I walk inside. In the middle of the room, a high, arched window beckons. I'm a moth, drawn to the glow that fills the sky.

Beneath me, Las Vegas glitters. Lights flash, so many colors. It blends together in a swirl. Way, way, way far down, people climb into limos and climb out of them again. Everything's in motion. Not far from here, a black pyramid fires light into the sky. It's like a science fiction novel opened up and some crazy shit's about to happen.

At the edges of the light, shadows flicker and I realize it must be birds. Or bats. Or maybe it's beaming people down, I don't know. But I have the best view of it. I could read by it, except my eyes are blurry and I left my library card at home.

Arden's hands touch my hips, then slide around my waist. She fills the space behind me. Her warmth feeds me; I lean into it. Into her. Her body is a miracle, strong and beautiful against me. I close my eyes—I'm not drifting. I'm absorbing. The sound of her voice and the shape of her, pressed against me. The way she shifts weight from foot to foot. How she draws circles on my back, over and over. Her touch spirals on, marking me without marking me.

"We're gonna be there tomorrow," she says, her voice buzzing on my skin.

With a smile, I say, "Yeah, we are."

"You wanna celebrate tonight?"

Turning in her arms, I steal a kiss from her teasing mouth. "Yeah, I do."

I'm not suave. I'm not graceful. I don't belong in a place like this, with a girl like her, and I don't give a damn. Backing her toward the bed, I have to be careful. This isn't a movie, but it doesn't have to be a disaster, either.

When we sink into that cloud of bed, she pulls me down for a kiss. Finally, I'm allowed to sink my fingers into the wilds of her hair again. My lips brush her chin; my nose grazes against hers. This is the quietest place in the world, the space inside her arms. Somewhere to think, and be. Somewhere to die, but I won't. It would be cruel. I got the miracle, so I have a list now.

One more kiss. One more day. All the rest, after that. I won't die here in Arden's arms.

But I could. It would be so peaceful.

# (CHECK OUT)

**In the morning, I wake to find myself alone. There's a** note on the bedside table that says *Ran to store, back in a few.* As I swallow down lukewarm water (cold makes my stomach clench), I stare at Arden's handwriting. It's dark, thick—not in cursive. It's like the lettering in a comic book, all action and strong.

It surprises me. I go back to the note again as I finish the strawberries we ordered from room service late last night. The note wavers in my hand; I trace the lines of her letters with my knuckle. Everything about Arden is sweet, and round and gentle. But when she writes, she claims the page and fills it completely. A secret glimpse of her insides? I think so. The page doesn't smell like her, but these sheets do. My skin does.

I owe her so much for starting over with me.

Except, I'm not all the way started over, am I?

The room phone is heavy when I pick it up. I have to read the instructions twice to figure out the whole outside line dealie. A call this complicated makes me feel stupid, but it's a passing sensation. So what? It's just a phone. Pressing numbers carefully, I hold my breath when the line rings. After three, I think it's going to go to voice mail.

Then suddenly, my mother's wary voice says, "Hello?"

Normally she doesn't answer unknown callers, but this one is probably coming up with the name of the hotel. Who knows, maybe she won a paid vacation for two to Las Vegas. Maybe she and Lynne can get away from the Waffle n' Steak for a while. Do some serious blackjack therapy, see some shows, throw some panties. I almost feel bad that she's not getting that trip. Almost.

Pressing a cold hand to my forehead, I stare at the remains of my berries. "The car's in Amaranth."

"Dylan?" she asks.

"Yeah, Ma, it's me," I say. I wait.

I hear her breathing on the other line. Thin, sharp inhalation. Short, hard exhalation. I remember laying next to her at night, when I was very little.

When I was afraid of lightning, or nightmares, or the moon (I was afraid of the moon; when it rose full in my window, I couldn't breathe), I climbed into her bed. Folded against her, I was so safe. She was so soft. Her face was beautiful when she slept, the tension smoothed out of it. She changed rooms with me after a while because she said she couldn't sleep with me kicking her shins all damned night.

I'm not ashamed to say I want that again, that before. That time when she was the most beautiful woman in the world and I loved her until I overflowed with it. She's my mom, and I can forgive everything, I can. A fist clutches my heart, ready to squeeze or set free. I don't know which yet. I hope, I'm a stupid little hoping thing.

"Where the fuck is Amaranth?" she asks. "And where the fuck are you? The school called, wanting to know when you were coming back to register, you little shit. I thought you were gonna register."

She says it like it's not her fault. Like I wasn't humiliated at the desk trying to register *alone*. The anger flares up, but then . . . it dies. I rationalize: she has a right to be angry. I did take her car and leave her stranded with no notice. God, I am *full* of goodness and light this morning. I just want her to love me again.

"Well?" she demands.

At first, I think I'm crying. My face is hot, but when I touch it, it's not wet. Am I sad? Ashamed? I don't even know anymore. My whole body flexes. I'm one agonized twist, and I roll back into bed. "I'm sorry. I wasn't thinking."

She snorts, and I hear her relay this information to somebody. Lynne, no doubt. Or maybe Bobby. Maybe he drummed up that two hundred dollars, and she welcomed him home. To me, she says, "Where are you?"

"Las Vegas," I say.

"You'd better be fucking kidding," she says. Flinty. Already calculating the distance between here and there. "Where are you really?"

My throat closes. "Las Vegas, for real. I'm with a friend. I'm fine."

"Well you'd better find a way to get your fine ass back home.

Don't think I'm coming out there after you."

Clutching the phone until my knuckles ache, I pull the covers closer. They smell like Arden, clean. So clean. I bury my face in them and I don't cry. Instead, I drain. I feel it, at the crown of my head, rushing down through my throat, through my belly, all the way down my useless, aching legs. The soles of my feet tingle when it finally leaves me.

People are who they are. There was never going to be a last minute transformation. My mother was never gonna sit at my graduation, and break down to reveal: she was hard all this time just to save her soft heart. All the horrible things she said were just a shield; she made me drive to my own appointments because she couldn't bear to see me suffer. Et cetera, et cetera, infinity.

People want families to fit together perfectly, no matter what, but sometimes they don't. It's when we keep trying to force them together that we get hurt.

Her life didn't go as planned. Neither did mine. We are who we are, and I can live with that. (It probably doesn't sound like it, but I promise you—I feel better now. I do.) I cover my eyes with my hand and I say, "I'll see you later, okay?"

My mother hangs up on me.

# (ALMOST NOWHERE)

**Leaving Las Vegas doesn't have the same glitter as** meeting it. In the daylight, the town is a little dirty, a little lonely. I'm not, though. This car is closer quarters; it's better than the Escalade because I'm right next to Arden; she's right next to me.

My hand keeps straying to my head. There's a buzzy emptiness in it. I keep waiting for it to twist up, freak out, start backtracking, something, but it doesn't. I said what I said to my mother, and that's it. But it just doesn't. My head is clear.

I lean into Arden, my head on her shoulder as she drives, and chase her fingers with mine. The haze has receded. I think the desert burned it off. Everything is good. I feel *good*. Glancing up at her, I'm happy to see that Arden wears a faint smile, too.

"Whatcha thinking?" I ask, stroking my thumb through her palm.

Her smile widens. "I don't know. Just random stuff."

"Like what?"

"I don't have a favorite song," she says. She sounds a little amazed when she admits it. "Or a favorite movie, or a favorite book."

"Me either. There's too many. How do you pick a favorite?"

"Exactly!" Her whole body shakes when she gets excited. She pounds the wheel and her curls dance and she comes alive. "Like, I can list *some* of my favorites. But I need different stuff for different occasions."

"My favorite book is A Steamy Romance Novel," I joke. It's junk loot in the game, and I start to laugh. "Remember the first time you pickpocketed one of those things?"

"I still have it!" Arden beams at me. "I have all kinds of dumb stuff in my bank."

"Me too," I say. Virtual banks. Imaginary riches. Settling against her again, I smile crookedly. "I bet that Mallet of

Zul'Farrak comes in handy again."

"Oh yeah, my Violet Signet, too."

"You remember our first day in Burning Crusade? That's what this reminds me of."

Arden leans over the wheel, nodding. "I know, right?"

That means nothing to you, I'm thinking. So okay, World of Warcraft gets new content every couple years, in an expansion pack. Basically, it's new stuff to do so people keep playing. The Burning Crusade was the very first one, a whole new planet to explore.

You had to be, I think, level 60 to get into the new stuff. Maybe 55. Whatever—I dinged first, meaning I hit the level cap before Arden did. Not by much, and it didn't matter anyway. No way was I going in there without her. It was a big deal; we wanted to walk through the portal to the new world together.

Once we did, we stood on a terrace, looking out at Hellfire Peninsula.

Speeding down this barren highway, into the Mojave Desert, I think I know where Warcraft got some of their ideas. At angles, this desert is red like Mars. Like California, when the fires consume the sky. Dark mountains frame the horizon, but the land is red. Dusty. Tire tracks crisscross the side of the road, evidence that some people drove out here in something besides a sedan.

All the plants are greyish green, low to the ground and spiky. I haven't seen one cactus yet, but I don't care. Above us, the sky is bluer than it's ever been. Deep, rich—the shade I expected to see at the Mississippi River. There's no traffic, no street lights. No people, no houses. There's nothing here but heavens and earth, the road the only proof people have been here before at all.

The heat presses from the outside in. The air conditioner struggles to keep up, but I can feel it losing. I like this place. Quietly, to myself, I can admit. I don't think we're going to find anything here but more desert, but I like it all the same.

I pull Arden's hand to my lips and kiss it. I lay it against my cheek and I ask, "You wanna have our last fight now, or later?"

She stiffens a little. "I don't want to fight at all."

"After we find the ship," I say, "and we have our news conference and we spend the night together drinking champagne and eating caviar, I want you to call your dad. I want you to go home."

"Fuck him. No."

Though I approve of the sentiment, I can't get behind it. Not now. "He wants you back. He canceled all your shit, Arden."

"Because he's an asshole," she says blackly.

Reaching for her phone, I admit I did a bad thing. I turned it on after I called my mom. I wanted to see. If Concrete Blocks was made out of the same stuff. If he was, I could run away with Arden, keep her forever, never look back. Why not? Why not? People run away to California all the time.

So I listened; I listened to all the messages. At first, I saved them because I didn't want to get caught. But when I was done, I knew there was a better reason to keep them.

"Don't be mad," I say, playing voice mails I heard, that I think she ought to. Speaker lights up; Concrete Blocks' voice fills the car.

"I don't know what's gotten into you, David—"

Arden is wounded; I swear to god, she'd look less broken if I hit her or something. Just thinking that makes me sick; I can't imagine raising a hand to do anything to her, but love her. Not ever. Never.

So I hit Delete. That one's not important by itself; it's all of them, listened to one after the other. That's what's important.

Number two: "I haven't called the police. I don't want this to be an issue." Delete.

"I know it's been a hard couple of years—" Delete.

Arden's voice trembles. "Why are you doing this to me?"

"You could have talked to me. You didn't have to run away. Dav—" Delete.

"Stop," Arden says.

I don't. I hold the phone out of her reach. The next message cues—it starts with a long silence. Then finally, simply, Concrete Blocks says, "Come home. Come home, *Arden*."

No delete. Not this time. I thought Arden might want to keep that. Maybe forever. I hang up the phone and give it back. It's not mine. It never was. Neither is Arden, and I have to put her back better than I found her.

Agitated, Arden pulls over. She throws the car in Park and turns to me. When I see her face, I think I should have waited until after we found the ship to have this talk. Anger and fear and frustration rise off her in waves. Red splotches stain her face. Her voice vibrates on my skin; she's so angry.

"What's the matter with you? Are you trying to break my heart?"

Clasping her face in my hands, I look at her. I really look. She's scared and sad and I'm finally okay for once. I don't mind reassuring her, because she's just a couple steps back from me. She'll catch up. She'll be okay. Fingertips on her temples, eye to eye with her, I say, "I want to be honest with you, okay? I want you to listen and to hear me."

"Dylan," she protests.

"Give him a chance," I tell her, my voice thickening. "And if he fucks it up, then blame me. And you can, all right? It's okay. Because I'm gonna be the one who stays, Arden. That doesn't change. I'm gonna be the one who stays."

She cries. I hold her. She holds me; I cry, too.

# (0)

**The Salton Sea is a grey, imposing lake, and its shores** are abandoned. At least, they are where we stop. Long stretches of warning signs and sunburned cans litter the shore. I can't call it a beach, not really. Beaches have balls and lifeguards and suntan lotion. None of that here. I don't even see any birds.

Once upon a time, people thought this place was gonna be an oasis. They built resorts all around it and got movie stars to come. But stuff flows into the sea and nothing flows out. The salt built up, the fish mostly died, and now it's just a dead lake in the middle of the desert. If Iturbe's ship hadn't gotten stuck in the river shallows, this is where he would have ended up: trapped in the desert all the same.

When I slide out of the car, I stumble. The wind rushes past, hot like somebody's blowing a hair dryer at me. Holding out my hands, I walk into it like I'm new or blind. Turning slowly, I marvel. The wind is like a blow dryer, turned up high. I've never felt anything like it.

"Are you okay?" Arden asks.

"I'm awesome," I say, turning my face to the sky and the sun. "The wind is hot."

She nods, smiling at me curiously. "Weird, huh?"

"It's cool," I say.

"Nope," she replies. "Hot."

Stupid joke, and I laugh at it. Breaking out her phone, Arden pulls up the map she saved from all her satellite searches. There are GPS coordinates to follow. Once the app is running, she hands the phone to me. "Lead the way, Dylan."

She marked the teardrop shape, and the path is easy to follow. We walk out due west from the lake. Away from the water. Away from old, rusted buildings that are slowly falling back into the sand. One day, there will be nothing here. Just water saltier than the ocean, and sand. Mountains. Sky. Wind that sears when it eddies around you.

My heart pounds in a hard, uneven stroke, and I don't care. Somewhere in these sands, a ghost ship sails. Baskets decorate its decks, full of stolen pearls. So many, there are ropes of them. Loops. Hung from the mast, they'd loop along the sails, once, twice, three times even.

"Who should we call first when we find it?" Arden asks.

Considering this, I say, "I don't know. I was thinking we could tweet it."

"With pictures," Arden agrees.

"Yup, pix or it didn't happen."

The ground isn't as smooth as I thought a desert would be. It's constantly moving, thick roots hidden to trip you, then exposed, to do the same. Sweat soaks me. I'm that prize race-horse again, rivers of sweat, about to be put down. You know what, though? That horse ran as fast and as hard as it could.

"You know what pisses me off?" I ask. "I haven't seen even one tumbleweed. What do I gotta do to see tumbleweed?"

Helpfully, Arden says, "I saw some on the way to Las Vegas."

"Pix or it didn't happen," I mutter.

The phone leads us deeper into the desert. By deeper, I mean when I look back, I know where the car is, but I can't see it. Nor the Salton Sea, nor the signs, nor the debris. This is the literal middle of nowhere, but a safe version of it. One where we have GPS to walk us right back to civilization if it gets too scary.

Stopping, I reach for Arden's hand. The wind blasts us, hot and insisting. "Hold up," I say, because I want to listen.

Sand slides against sand, a whisper that echoes in every direction. There are no voices, no music. There's nothing but our breath and the breath of the wind. Beneath the sun, I'm burning and bubbling up, but for just this moment, I don't hurt at all.

This moment, this second, is worth the whole trip. This is what I hope I dream about from now on. Whispering sands, and Arden standing close to me, her hand in mine. All those miles behind us, arguments and jokes, new places, terrifying places. The biggest ball of twine, and my best, new, first kiss with her. One night in the state park; another all luxe at the top of Las Vegas. I don't want to cry anymore; I'm not afraid. I just am, right now; the two of us, we exist and that's enough.

"You okay?" she asks, drawing closer.

"Almost there," I say. The moment's over, but it's not gone. I wear it around my shoulders; it slips onto my fingers like rings. I tug to get her moving again.

Over a rocky ledge, and into a cool shadow, we follow the GPS as it points the way. The red line slowly turns green, brightening, then flashing. Then at once it turns white, with a little trumpety fanfare. This is the place. This is what Arden found on the satellite maps.

I expected to be elated. Or disappointed. But what I am is peaceful. With the wind whispering on the sand, it's peaceful. The desert breaks through the constant cold on my skin, and I sink to sit. We crossed two thousand miles for this. For the first time in my life, I'm satisfied.

Arden turns; we both search. I trail my fingers through hot sand and squint up at the sky. This band of exposed stone makes a nice wall. A shady place to sit and play. Scooping up handfuls of sand, I let the grains slip between my fingers. It's too dry for sand castles. If I draw in it, the shapes blow away almost instantly. So I dig, and I weigh, and I am happy.

"I think . . . ," Arden says, turning in a circle. She looks bereft, dust lining the streaks on her face. "I think what I saw was this ledge."

"It's okay," I tell her.

Sinking next to me, Arden covers her face. This, I hate. Because I'm exactly where I want to be, and it's really obvious she's not. Maybe she believed more than I did. I don't think she's crying, though she doesn't raise her face. More like, she crashed, and now she has to put herself back together. She has to go home and be alive and do all the things you do when you breathe and your heart beats.

Rubbing my shoulder against hers, I raise another handful of sand. It's like a kiss when it spills between my fingers. Though I know Arden's wounded, I'm not. I'm just not. We made it. We're here in an impossible place that never existed before. Just like the world in the game, I saw it through glass—but now it's real.

As the last of the sand drains from my hands, my heart skips. It jumps, it twitches like a living thing. All these acrobatics, because something remains in my palm.

"Arden," I say.

Her reply is muffled. "What?"

"Arden, look," I say.

A burst of energy fills me. Scrambling to her, I pin her down and straddle her hips. Electricity zings through my veins. It activates me, and I laugh, oh god, I laugh. The world shifts beneath me, and so does Arden. Her body wriggles; she tries to sit up.

I plant one hand in the middle of her chest to hold her still. Then I hold it out, right above her head. Just far enough away that her eyes cross when she tries to look at it.

One perfect pearl.

# (0)

**You already know what happens. Maybe you're not ready** to admit it. I understand that. Maybe it'll make you feel better if I tell you that we kissed, and we had dinner in Palm Springs. We made plans to see each other again; I made her write her name on my skin. I cried when she left, and she came back an hour later for one more kiss. Does that make you feel better?

After she's gone, I spread the porch doors in my room. She gave me what was left of the cash, and I rented a run-down cabana near the shores of a lifeless sea. The doors open onto the desert; they let all that good heat in. The sky is forever. The sand is forever. I sit there and watch the sun go down, and I don't cry.

There's a place between hope and despair. If I still despaired, I'd cry. I'd still be raging against the dying of the light—I love that poem, I do, but I don't feel it anymore. I don't feel it when Death Cab for Cutie makes promises to follow me into the dark—that belongs to someone else, now. It all belongs to someone else now, and that's all right.

We don't know what we are while we still are. Maybe some of us get a glimpse of it. I'm pretty sure Beyoncé has a grasp on her place in the social consciousness. The Prince of Cambridge knows that one day, he's the king, the next link in a chain of time that stretches back—but forward, too.

The Appalachians are old for mountains. The Rockies are young. They're real, I can tell you that, because I've seen them both. They're more real than you or me, because they'll last. That's a fact that lives in that place between hope and despair. In the place without fear, without hurt, without hesitation.

You're going to turn the next page, because you still have hope. You hope there's a little something more, and it's nothing personal. People do it at the end of every book. I think that's why publishers put in all those extra pages. So you have a chance to shuffle and flip through them while it sinks in. It's over. The trip is done.

You know it's over, but you're going to turn the page anyway.

I'll tell you right now, there's nothing on it.

**(0)**

JOIN THE

# Epic Reads
## COMMUNITY

### THE ULTIMATE YA DESTINATION

◀ **DISCOVER** ▶
your next favorite read

◀ **MEET** ▶
new authors to love

◀ **WIN** ▶
free books

◀ **SHARE** ▶
infographics, playlists, quizzes, and more

◀ **WATCH** ▶
the latest videos

www.epicreads.com